THE PASSENGER

Fifth Draft

1/24/05

Copyright © 2006 by Jamie Sonderman and Michael Zawacki
ISBN# 0-9754074-2-2

All rights reserved. No part of this book may be reproduced without the permission of the publishers.

Elitist Publications 487 W Alexandrine, Third floor Detroit, MI 48201
www.elitistpublications.com

PRINTED IN THE UNITED STATES OF AMERICA
Printed at N.W. Coughlin & Company - Livonia, Michigan
www.nwcoughlin.com

This is a work of fiction. Any resemblance to actual persons, living or dead, is purely coincidental.

Cover Art by: Eric Livingston www.cellar8design.com

www.thoughtcollide.com

Other Books from:

Killing Molly
by Eric C. Novack

The Silent Burning
by Ryan Bartek

Upcoming books:

Summer 2006- *Wendy* by Josh Malerman
www.thehighstrung.com

Fall 2006- *Incubus Succubus* by L.A. Nantz
www.v3in.com

Jamie Sonderman,

Mike Zawacki

FADE IN:

INT. A ROOM - EARLY MORNING

Dolly shot of the hardwood floor. Sunlight stretches across the floor as we slowly follow it. Shouts and moans of pleasure and pain as well as scraping and scuffing can be heard O.S. Soon the sounds stop. We come to rest on a lightly pulsating hand with a large nail driven through it, Jesus Christ style. A small pool of blood has formed around the hand.

INT. HOUSE OF NINE - NIGHT

Hard driven music erupts. C.U. of blackness. Slow pull out. As we pull back pulsing light reveals itself with intermingling moving shadows. After a long strange surreal show, the pulsing lights and shadows are eventually revealed to be HUNDREDS OF PEOPLE dancing in a club. They are silhouetted by the lights.

INT. HOUSE OF NINE - NIGHT

The night club is dark except for the narrow flashing lights. The music pounds. We find JOHN among the many Clubbers. John looks around the crowded club three girls catch his eye.

TAYLOR Stands against a railing. She looks at her watch and looks around as if she were waiting for someone.

LYDIA is sitting at a small table looking about hopefully.

ZINN stands by the bar looking frustrated and unapproachable. She looks like the demon lover that every man fantasizes about being with at least once in their lives.

John straightens his clothes and picks his way through the crowded club and towards Taylor. While on his way they make eye contact, but only for a moment.

                JOHN
  So...
    (Beat)
  Have you ever noticed that when you first meet someone in a club or something for the first time you always start each sentence with the word "So"?

                TAYLOR
  It's probably because you're nervous, or just aren't sure of yourself or what you are about to say. Maybe you're nervous because you aren't sure of the other person. Like, maybe they're psycho or something.
    (Beat)
  I do it all the time.

John smiles.

Taylor lets out a short, girlish scream. She embraces JANICE. Janice is pretty and is dressed in the uniform of a modern club patron.

              TAYLOR (CONT'D)
  Hey! How are you!

                JANICE
  Great! Any luck with Mark?

    Taylor's face clouds up.

                TAYLOR

No, I haven't seen him anywhere.

Janice nods knowingly.

JANICE
Well... are you going to introduce me to your friend?

TAYLOR
He and I were just getting acquainted. What was your name?

JOHN
John.

TAYLOR
Hi John, this is Janice.

John and Janice shake hands and their eyes meet for a moment.

JANICE
Nice to meet you John.

John smiles and puts his attention back on Taylor. Taylor looks him in the eyes.

JANICE (CONT'D)
I think I'll go dance. See you two soon.

Janice leaves for the dance floor.

JOHN
Who was that?

TAYLOR
She is the friend I was waiting for.

JOHN
Don't you want to hang around her?

TAYLOR

                    No.
                         (beat)
                    I'm pretty good right here.

                         John smiles.

INT. THE METROPOLIS CAFE - NIGHT

John and Taylor are sitting on a sofa already engaged
in conversation. They are laughing.

                    TAYLOR
          ...Well it's hard to meet someone. It's
          really complicated. There are so many
          things you have to consider. First
          you have to find someone who is also
          looking for someone. Then you have to be
          attracted to that person. That person has
          to be attracted to you. You have to be
          somewhat compatible - the same interests,
          hobbies...
               (beat)
          ...music seems to be important. The
          situation has to be right for you to
          actually meet that person. You just can't
          walk up to someone these days and say "Hi"
          or they'll think your like...

She makes quote signs with her hands.

                    TAYLOR (CONT'D)
          ..."hitting on them". As if that is so
          bad. It's like, the worst thing these
          days to want to get to know an interesting
          stranger.
               (beat)
          See, we've gotten this far. Yay us!

John chuckles.

                    TAYLOR (CONT'D)

What was I talking about?

                    JOHN
How hard it is...

               JOHN AND TAYLOR
...to find someone.

                    TAYLOR
Once you've met this person and asked them
out, they have to say yes. You have to
have the free time to do it.

                    JOHN
You have to live a reasonable distance
from each other.

                    TAYLOR
Exactly. Once you're together you have to
go along at the same pace in order for the
relationship to work. If one person falls
in love faster than the other it scares
the other one away. If you get all that
right then you're pretty much home free.

                    JOHN
Okay, good. Where do you live?

                    TAYLOR
Birmingham.

                    JOHN
Well, there's one thing - I live in
Ferndale. That's just a few miles away.

                    TAYLOR
Right, but then there's marriage. You
have to maintain that special relationship
and fall in love...
          (beat)
...whatever that is. You have to survive

that first fight. I'm surprised that
people get married at all. It has got
to be next to impossible to maintain a
relationship. I have enough trouble with
my car. Everyone changes with time. If
you and your partner don't change in the
same way...
(beat)
...you're screwed. You have to
communicate. That's not easy. I'm not
gonna get married unless everything is
perfect and I'm sure. Love is tough.

John puts on an outrageously overdone French accent, gesturing around the cafe.

JOHN
Ah, l'amoure! For me she is easy. I
could have any woman I want. But I am
stuck with you!

They both laugh.

CUT TO:

EXT. CITY STREET - NIGHT

The two are walking toward their cars. John checks his watch.

JOHN
I've got to go to work in four hours. I
feel like life is passing me by. I'm
constantly working. That's why I went out
tonight. To do something different

JOHN
(CONT'D)
and see what's out there. I would have
done anything tonight! I would have gone
bungee jumping with gay Nazis wearing bras

over their eyes like bugs.

> TAYLOR
> Well, I'm glad that you came out tonight and met me instead of bungee jumping Nazis.

The pair look into each others eyes and smile. They reach Taylor's car. Taylor leans her back against it. John leans in to kiss her. Taylor pulls away.

> TAYLOR (CONT'D)
> I'm... I'm sorry.

> JOHN
> No, it was too forward of me, I...

> TAYLOR
> No, it's not you! It's just... There's someone. Someone else.

> JOHN
> You mean you're seeing someone. Else.

Taylor looks down and nods.

> TAYLOR
> I had a really good time.

> JOHN
> Yeah, me too.

Taylor looks up to meet his gaze.

> TAYLOR
> Good night.

> JOHN
> Night.

Taylor gets into her car and drives away. John watches her go.

INT. JOHN'S OFFICE ELEVATOR - MORNING

John is standing in the back of the lift with two other gentleman and a lady. He's obviously distracted and out of sorts. The doors begin to close but before they can a briefcase slams into crack, re-opening the doors. In walks STEVE who takes his place next to John.

                    JOHN
Good morning sunshine, nice of you to drop in.

                    STEVE
You look like poo. What's up?

                    JOHN
I met a girl last night.

                    STEVE
Like a real girl? Or like a girl from Canada?

                    JOHN
No, jackass, a real girl. Her name is Taylor. She's got all the qualities I look for in a girl. She's pretty. She's smart. She's got a great sense of humor. We talked all night. I haven't been to bed.

                    STEVE
Ah, so it wasn't one of <u>those</u> first dates.

The elevator door pings and opens. The duo get off.

INT. JOHN'S OFFICE - MORNING

Many Cubicles. An old account poster hangs on the wall. It is for life insurance. It reads: "Life is for the living."

> STEVE
> So you met your dream girl. Why the long face?

INT. JOHNS CUBICAL - MORNING

There is a computer and lots of scattered papers. Some advertisement proposals and sketches hang from the low wall. Steve's head pokes over the partition.

> STEVE
> A boyfriend? And she led you on all night?

> JOHN
> Story of my life.

> STEVE
> She wants to leave him.

> JOHN
> How the hell do you know that?

> STEVE
> No girl will talk to you all night and not mention her boyfriend unless she's looking for someone else to give her the hot beef injection.

John throws up his hands.

> JOHN
> Why do I even talk to you about these things?

> STEVE
> No, seriously! You, my friend, were being taken out for a test drive.

> JOHN
> You're a font of inspiration, pal. Now quit bugging me. Anderson wants the paper

work for the Osterman account by noon or it's my ass.

Steve pops back into his cube. John works on his concept sketch for a bit but quickly stops, sitting and staring at a simple, printed sign which says "Bored Beyond Belief."

EXT. CAFE - EVENING

The after work crowd filters into the cafe.

INT. CAFE - EVENING

John walks up to the wait stand.

    MARTIN
Hi, how many?

    JOHN
Two.

    MARTIN
Okay, just a second.

Martin goes to clear a table. Something over John's shoulder catches his eye.

    MARTIN (CONT'D)
Hey T! Here on your day off?

    TAYLOR (O.S.)
Can't get enough of the place.

At the sound of Taylor's voice John's eyes widen. He turns around. Taylor is similarly surprised to see John. She smiles radiantly.

    JOHN
Hi.

    TAYLOR

Um... hi.

                    JOHN
And here I thought I'd never see you
again.

                    TAYLOR
Well, it was just a matter of time. I
work here.

                    JOHN
Better sooner than later.

                    TAYLOR
I'm meeting Janice, you remember her? You
want join us?

                    JOHN
I'd love to. I'm actually meeting someone
else here.

                    TAYLOR (TO MARTIN)
Make it four, baby.

                    MARTIN
Where should I put you?

                    TAYLOR
Back at table 14 - And 4 of the usual.

                    MARTIN
Non-smoking, right?

    Martin leads them back to their table.

                    JOHN
Everyone smokes these days. It's getting
to be a clichÈ.

                    TAYLOR
God, yes. It's the one thing that crosses
all subcultures.

                    JOHN
It's like they all go to "The Clichè
Store" and pick up their new addiction
along with their ultra baggy pants or
combat boots, or whatever.

John and Taylor sit down at their table.

                    TAYLOR
Exactly! It's the one iconic symbol of
rebellion they can all agree on. Nicotine
- "Uniting the surly and angstful".

                    JOHN
The cigarette companies are winning
big time. How is it possible in this
day and age to have a product that is
addictive to the user. That seems a
little underhanded. If a candy bar were
addictive no one would stand for it. Why
stop with cigarettes? Why not make yogurt
addictive? They'd make millions more a
year.

                    TAYLOR
They should just outlaw all drugs.

                    JOHN
I dunno. The lighter stuff seems kind
of... intriguing.

Taylor visibly bristles. John sees this and begins
to backpedal.

                    JOHN (CONT'D)
I mean I haven't tried it. They just make
it sound interesting.

                    TAYLOR
Trust me - none of it leads anywhere
people like you or I want to go. My... I

know people who got into that scene and it really messed them up.

                    JOHN
I'm sorry...

                    TAYLOR
No, it's okay. I didn't mean to come off all Nancy Regan on you. It's just a sore spot for me.

                    JOHN
Well then I'll take your word for it, Nancy.

They share a smile as Janice walks up to their table.

                    JANICE
Hey! Taylor rises and give Janice a hug.

   As she pulls away she gestures to
   Janice's earrings.

                    TAYLOR
Wow! I love these! Where did you get them?

                    JANICE
Crosswinds.

                    TAYLOR
Pricey!

                    JANICE
I decided to treat myself.

Taylor leans her head next to Janice, so that the earring dangles under her earlobe. She looks at John.

                    TAYLOR
          What do you think? Are they my color?

John seems slightly taken aback by this.

                    JOHN
          Yes, they, uh... they match your purse.

     Taylor and Janice sit.

                    TAYLOR
          I'll call Daddy and have him get me a
          pair.

Janice snickers. Steve steps up to the group and
holds out his arms to John.

                    STEVE
          Hey big, guy! So where's my hug?

                    JOHN (LAUGHING)
          Sit down, you ass!
               (to Janice and Taylor)
          This is Steve. Steve, this is Taylor and
          her friend Janice.

Hand shakes are exchanged.

                    JANICE
          So, John where are you from?

                    JOHN
          Ferndale.

                    JANICE
          Nice. Where do you live Steve?

                    STEVE
          With my parents.

He pauses for dramatic effect.

STEVE (CONT'D)
Yeah, I feel that times being what they are, it's impossible to live comfortably on ones own.

JOHN
Here we go.

STEVE
When our parents were getting started they didn't have the overhead we do now.

JANICE
Overhead?

STEVE
Yeah, look at all the expenses we have that they didn't. Car insurance, cable TV, cell phones, health insurance. Add this to maintaining and fueling your car and bam!! You're at home with the folks.

TAYLOR
I know a lot of my friends who have moved back home.

MARTIN
I just moved back home.

Martin delivers a tray full of steaming drinks and continues on his way.

JANICE
You sound like you've said all of this before.

JOHN
Steve's a big advocate of living with parents.

STEVE
Everyone needs a cause. Maybe one day

destiny or fate will strike and I'll win enough money to live in a place as nice as the one I'm at now, but until that happens I'm living at home.

                    JANICE
Do you believe in fate?

                    STEVE
Yeah, why not?

                    TAYLOR
You believe in a giant cosmic force that makes everything happen?

                    STEVE
Well, not exclusively. I think everything happens for a reason though.

                    JOHN
I don't know if I buy into that or not. Destiny, put simply, is the place you end up, your destination. It can't be predetermined. But everything you do, every decision you make, effects the place you go and the people you meet.

                    JANICE
But that's kind of like fate. If you didn't meet THAT person you wouldn't have been effected THAT way and your life would be different. Either a lot or a little. Think of how many decisions we make in a day that change our lives in some small way or another.

                    JOHN
True. Think of how those decisions change our friends' and families' lives as well.

                    STEVE
          Yeah, like, if your mother had decided to
          do her hair that day instead of playing
          softball she would have never met your
          father and things would be totally
          different.

                    TAYLOR
          Your parents met playing softball?

John shrugs.

                    STEVE
          What I'm saying is that these things
          happen everyday. Every decision we
          make changes our lives. Think of the
          path that led me here today. I moved
          in next door to John when I was 8, we
          became friends, we went to high school
          together, we both went off to the same
          college, we were room mates, we both
          went into advertising, he got me a job
          at McMann's, we happened to be here at
          the same time as you two. If any of
          those things were different I probably
          wouldn't be here. I might have a
          totally different job, have completely
          different friends, live in a different
          state. I would be a completely
          different person with different values
          and morals. Heck, I might have even had
          my own place and be making millions of
          dollars.
                    (beat)
          You prick! Look at what I could have had
          if it weren't for you!

                    JOHN
          Sorry to be holding you back.

EXT. CAFE PARKING LOT - NIGHT

John and Taylor walk side by side, followed by Steve and Janice, who are talking animatedly.

                    JOHN
Can I walk you to your car again?

Taylor looks into his eyes.

                    TAYLOR
Only if you promise to try and kiss me again.

                    JOHN
Deal.

John throws Steve his car keys.

                    JOHN (CONT'D)
Go warm it up for me big guy, I'm going accompany the lady to her car.

Steve and Janice head over to another part of the lot. John and Taylor arrive at her car. Taylor turns to face him. Taylor tentatively pulls John closer.

                    JOHN (CONT'D)
So what about... someone else?

                    TAYLOR
As of three days ago there's no one else.

John leans in and kisses her.

                    TAYLOR (CONT'D)
Can I get your number this time?

                    JOHN
248-176-5237. I'll talk to you tomorrow?

                    TAYLOR
Yeah, I'll give you a call.

> JOHN
> You're so pretty. Pretty girl.

Taylor kisses her index and middle finger and places them to John's lips. John smiles. She gets in her car. John helps her shut the door.

INT. JOHNS CAR - NIGHT

John is driving, Steve is in the passenger seat. A white four door car drives by John's car swerving dangerously close to John's front bumper. The white car pulls up next to a much nicer car. Zinn and MONICA, dressed very scantily, hang out of the passenger windows and begin yelling something garbled at the driver of the nice car.

> JOHN
> Hmmm... there's something you don't see very often.

> STEVE
> Nice rack on the short haired one.

INT. JOHN'S CUBICLE - DAY

John is talking on the phone, smiling like a man in love.

Steve walks by and stops, listening to John.

> JOHN
> Okay, I'll see you tonight. Bye.

> STEVE
> You've seen that girl almost every night this week. What gives?

> JOHN
> I don't know, we just like seeing each other.

                    STEVE
          Have you given her...

                    JOHN
          No. No injecting of hot beef has
          occurred. We just like spending time
          together.

                    STEVE
          So she's a lesbian?

John throws a balled up paper wad at Steve.

                    JOHN
          Out!

INT. JOHN'S APARTMENT - NIGHT

John Opens the door. Taylor enters - they kiss.

                    JOHN
          Hello! Let me get your coat.

Taylor shrugs her coat off, John goes to hang it up.

                    JOHN (CONT'D)
          This is pretty slick. Where'd you get it?

                    TAYLOR
          I designed it myself.

                    JOHN
          This is really good.

                    TAYLOR
          Thanks. I mean, hope it's good stuff.
          The coffee shop gig pays the bills but it
          just isn't my life. You know what I mean?

                    JOHN
          I... Yeah, I do.

There's an awkward pause between them.

              JOHN (CONT'D)
So... movie?

INT. JOHN'S APARTMENT - NIGHT

John and Taylor sit on the couch as the end credits to a movie roll. The remains of Chinese takeout are strewn about the table.

              TAYLOR
Wow... you're right. Willow is essentially just Star Wars.

              JOHN
But with more midgets.

Taylor giggles and starts getting her things together, getting ready to go.

              TAYLOR
Have you seen my phone?

              JOHN
Yeah, it was right by the door.

John gets up to retrieve the phone. Taylor spies a canvas barely poking above the back of the couch. Taylor slides it out from behind the couch. It's a half completed abstract. John comes back and sees her holding up the photo.

              JOHN (CONT'D)
Oh, you found the unfinished masterpiece.

              TAYLOR
It's nice. Why haven't you finished it?

              JOHN
I haven't really had time for that kind of stuff since I started at McMann. It's one

of those things where I can pay the bills
or play artist.

Taylor puts the painting back. John watches quietly as it vanishes behind the couch.

                  TAYLOR
  Good choice!

There's an uncomfortable pause. John finally breaks it, holding out Taylor's phone.

                  JOHN
  I called Bangkok. Hope you don't mind.

                  TAYLOR
  Eh. I get free calls after 8.

They move to the front door.

                  JOHN
  I'll walk you to your car.

Taylor opens the front door and shuts it quickly.

                  TAYLOR
  I can't go out there.

                  JOHN
  Huh? Why?

                  TAYLOR
  It's raining cats and dogs. Very unsafe weather for driving.

John opens the window and peaks out.

EXT. JOHN'S APARTMENT - NIGHT

It's utterly still and dry outside.

INT. JOHN'S APARTMENT - NIGHT

John closes the door, looking at Taylor.

> JOHN
> You're right. That's a damn monsoon.

Taylor drops her coat and wraps her arms around John.

> TAYLOR
> I'll... have to stay here. Tonight.

Their lips move closer.

> JOHN
> It would be uncivilized to send you out in that.

Their lips meet and they kiss, lightly at first, then with mounting passion and intensity. John slaps the light switch.

INT. JOHN'S CUBICAL - DAY

John's desk is immaculately clean. He sits playing with his "Bored Beyond Belief" sign. Steve pops his head over the side of the cubical.

> STEVE
> Something's different about you.

> JOHN
> Huh?

> STEVE
> Your face, it's different. You're happy.

> JOHN
> Last night was The Night.

> STEVE
> Oh?! Do tell.

> JOHN

You know a gentleman doesn't talk about such things.

> STEVE

That's never stopped you before.

> JOHN

Well, this one's different.

> STEVE

Oh?!
    (Beat)
That's cool.

> JOHN

Okay, so whenever I meet a girl, she'll be perfect in every way. Great body, good personality, goals, all that stuff. But then there's always something -- one thing --
That just blows it. Some piece of baggage. It's never a little thing. It's always some big bomb. Like, she's addicted to drugs, she has a kid, or two, or three. She's into some strange religion, like, pagan or she worships fairies...

> STEVE

Or she's married.

> JOHN

Hey, that was just the one time! Anyway, with Taylor I can't find any of these things. I keep waiting but it never comes. She's a great person. Is it possible that there is a completely perfect person in this world? Is it possible that I have her? Sure, we haven't agreed on every subject but that is a good quality in a girl.

STEVE
You sound serious.

JOHN
I don't know, I think I've found the one. I think I have found the girl I want to marry.

STEVE
Well, just be careful. She's on the rebound.

JOHN
What do you mean?

STEVE
Janice was talking about Taylor's ex-man. He was some high finance fancy pants. Six figure job, Mercedes, all that jazz.

JOHN
I don't know. I don't get that needy rebound thing from her. I'm really excited about her. I just hope I can be the man that makes her happy.

STEVE
Yeah, coming off a six figure main squeeze, you got a tough row to hoe before you rate husband material.

John swats at Steve.

JOHN
Man, get off it! I'm not saying I want to marry her tomorrow. I'm all about taking it slow.

STEVE
You know what Barney Rubble said about marriage.

JOHN
What's that?

STEVE
When a guy puts a wedding ring on his wife's finger it turns on a radar that allows her to read his mind.

INT. JOHN'S APARTMENT - NIGHT

John is talking on the phone.

TAYLOR (O.S.)
My dad got me an interview to work for a fashion designer!

JOHN
That's great!

TAYLOR (O.S.)
No! It's terrible!

JOHN
What?! I thought this is what you wanted to do!

TAYLOR (O.S.)
But... what if I screw it up?
    (Beat)
Oh, I don't think I'm gonna go. I'm not ready yet.

JOHN
Nonsense, I've seen your stuff. It's good. I think you should go.

TAYLOR
You think I'm good enough?

JOHN
Hell yeah!

TAYLOR
But all I would be doing is like getting the coffee and delivering designs and stuff. That's stupid. I want to design, not deliver coffee.

JOHN
But you got to get your foot in the door. It's all up from there.

TAYLOR
You think?

JOHN
When is your interview?

TAYLOR
Tomorrow at one thirty.

JOHN
Good. Call me right after and tell me how it went.

Silence from the other end of the line.

JOHN (CONT'D)
Taylor?

TAYLOR
What if she ask's me a hard question? What if I don't know the answer?

John throws up his hands and rolls his eyes.

JOHN
Okay.
    (Beat)
I'm gonna come over and I'll ask you some questions.

TAYLOR
You're gonna come over? What about work

tomorrow?

                    JOHN
It's okay. I'll be right over.

INT. JOHN'S CUBICAL - DAY

Steve leans on John's desk. John's desk clock reads 2:15.

                    STEVE
Boy, you look like hell.

                    JOHN
Yeah, I was up most of the night coaching Taylor for an interview today. We'll see how she does.

The telephone rings. John looks his phone.

                  JOHN (CONT'D)
That's her. John picks up the phone.

                  TAYLOR (O.S.)
I got the job!

                    JOHN
You did?! Wonderful!

                  TAYLOR (O.S.)
Yeah, no more slinging coffee for mopey goth brats!

                    JOHN
Alright!

                  TAYLOR (O.S.)
Tonight I take you out to dinner! I couldn't have done this without you.

                    JOHN
Tonight then. Dinner.

                    TAYLOR (O.S.)
          Hey, I gotta call my father. I'll see you
          tonight. Bye!

                    JOHN
          Bye, pretty girl.

INT. JOHN'S CAR - EVENING

                    JOHN
          Are you gonna tell me where we're going or
          what?

Taylor smiles mischievously.

                    TAYLOR
          You'll see.

John puts his hand on her knee. Taylor Smiles and
kisses her two fingers and touches John's lips.

EXT. RESTAURANT - NIGHT

Taylor and John walk through the front door of an
upscale restaurant.

INT. RESTAURANT - NIGHT

John and Taylor walk into the lobby. They are met
by MAURINE, Taylor's mother. Taylor's mother gives
Taylor a big hug.

                    MAURINE
          Hi sweety!

                    TAYLOR
          Mom, this is John.

John starts to extend his hand as Maurine gives him
a hug as well. John looks slightly surprised and
slowly pats her on the back.

> MAURINE
> Should we get seating for four or five?

> TAYLOR
> Just four, mom. I haven't heard from Mark.

Maurine looks dejected but quickly perks herself up as she leads Taylor and John inside.

> MAURINE
> Well, come on, your father's at the table already. Knowing him, he's probably already ordered!

Maurine looks back to John and loudly stage whispers to Taylor.

> MAURINE (CONT'D)
> He's cuter than Craig.

> TAYLOR
> Mom!!!

DISSOLVE TO:

INT. RESTAURANT - NIGHT, LATER

The table is set with a very hearty meal. ED, Taylor's father sits at the head of the table. MAURINE Taylor's mother sits across from him.

> ED
> So, John, What is it you do?

> JOHN
> Well, I am in advertising. McMann.

> ED
> Advertising, eh? Remind me to talk to you later.

                    JOHN
          I... okay.

                    ED
          Okay. John stares back, confused.

                    ED (CONT'D)
          Well go on! Eat! Your whoositmawhatsit's
          getting cold!

John smiles bemusedly and tucks in.

INT. RESTAURANT - NIGHT, LATER

Everyone is pretty well stuffed. The waiter comes
with the check.

Ed goes to reach for it, but Taylor swats his hand
away.

                    TAYLOR
          Daddy, don't you dare! This is my treat.

Ed feigns indignation.

                    ED
          What?! You expect me to bankrupt my own
          kids? They'll send Protective Services
          after me!

Ed reaches for the bill again. Taylor giggles.

                    TAYLOR
          I mean it!

Ed relents and Taylor takes the bill.

                    MAURINE
          Thank you for dinner, sweety.

                    TAYLOR
          No, thank you. Both of you.

Ed huffs and puffs at this display of girly emotion. He turns to John and gives him a knowing look.

> ED
> Tell you what. Let's go bring the cars around while the ladies pat each other on the back.

John nods. The men get up and leave.

INT. PARKING GARAGE - NIGHT

Ed and John make their way down a row of parked cars.

> ED
> Saaaaay.... Look at that. Ed takes a detour over to a '68 Mustang.

> ED (CONT'D)
> What a beauty! 1968 Ford Mustang.

Ed leans down to look under the car.

> ED (CONT'D)
> Looks like her underside's a little dinged up.

John stands by, saying nothing, as Ed stands up.

> ED (CONT'D)
> We just got a new lift in the garage. Give me and hour with that puppy and I'd have that undercarriage pretty as a picture. You a car man, John?

> JOHN
> Not really. I mean they're great, and I can appreciate the craftsmanship of something like the Mustang here, but I never had the chance to, uh, explore them as a field. Is that what you do?

ED
Cars are my passion. Fixing them up, getting them to run smooth. Best feeling in the world.

JOHN
Must come in handy having a mechanic in the family.

Ed eyes John, who immediately grows flustered.

JOHN (CONT'D)
Not that... I'm not saying... I mean, she's...

Ed laughs and claps John on the shoulder.

ED
So, you're in advertising, huh?

John is clearly relieved by the change of subject.

JOHN
That's right.

ED
You know, I've been looking at different agencies. I've been thinking on changing what we've got. Maybe I'll give yours a call.

John looks at the car.

JOHN
Uh, hey. Yeah. That would be great.

ED
McMann you say?

JOHN
Yeah.

They arrive at John's car.

              ED
You know John, you seem like you got a good head on your shoulders. Taylor certainly likes you.

              JOHN
Thank you, sir.

              ED
You got a good job too. You like your job?

              JOHN
It's... yeah. I like my job.

              ED
I'm not much of a hard case, but I gotta say, I get a little... squirely when it comes to my girl.

              JOHN
I can understand that. She's a terrific lady.

              ED
You two seem pretty serious.

              JOHN
We... uh...

Ed cuts him off with a wave of his hand.

              ED
Now I want you to remember something. You need to keep your priorities straight. If you're serious, it's very important that you keep her comfortable and happy. When I was your age, I stumbled on that from time to time. And what I've learned

is you've got to keep your priorities straight. No getting distracted. You know what I mean?

                    JOHN
          Yes, sir I do. Absolutely.

                    ED
          Alrighty. I'm over there.

Ed gestures a few spots down.

                    ED (CONT'D)
          Let's go get the gals.

EXT. RESTAURANT - NIGHT

John pulls up to the front door of the restaurant. Taylor and Maurine are waiting out front. Ed pulls up shortly after John in a perfectly restored '59 'Vette. Taylor hugs her parents.

                    MAURINE
          Thank you again for dinner sweety.

                    TAYLOR
          Anytime, mom. Bye Daddy.

Taylor hugs her dad. Ed and John shake hands. Everyone gets into their respective cars and leaves.

INT. JOHN'S CAR - NIGHT

                    TAYLOR
          So, what did you think of my folks?

                    JOHN
          Your mom's a sweetheart. And your dad...
          Your dad's a trip.

                    TAYLOR
          Yeah, he can be a handful. He really

liked you, though.

                JOHN
I hope so. I always get nervous around mechanics.

                TAYLOR
Huh?

                JOHN
Some people are weirded out by clowns. Mechanics make me feel... less manly, somehow.

                TAYLOR
Ha! You think my dad's a mechanic?

                JOHN
Well.... I mean, what does he do?

                TAYLOR
He owns Checker Moving Company. You know "the moving people"? He has a fleet of antique cars. He spends almost as much time on them as the moving business.

                JOHN
Oh.
     (Beat)
OH! Oh my!

                TAYLOR
What is it?

                JOHN
I think he offered me an account.

                TAYLOR
Did you take it?

                JOHN
Well, I thought he worked in a garage. I

didn't think the firm would be
Interested. And I'm just a grunt -
I don't run accounts.

> TAYLOR

Dad's been looking for an agency for quite
some time. Maybe he could give you a leg
up.

John is quiet for a beat or two. Then...

> JOHN

So your dad owns Checker...

> TAYLOR

Yeah.

> JOHN

...and you work at a coffee shop?!

> TAYLOR

I don't want to sponge off my parents.
And I meet all sorts of fashion type
people at the cafe. Helps me keep my
street cred.

John laughs.

> JOHN

You're something else, pretty girl.

INT. LARRY'S OFFICE - MORNING

> LARRY

Oh, Hey John! Just the man I'm looking
for. Can you come in here for a bit?

> JOHN

I have to call Anderson about the proofs
for the Osterman ads, can I get right back
to you?

                    LARRY
          That call can wait my boy. Have you heard
          of the Checker Moving Company?

                    JOHN
          Uh, yeah. That's...

Ed turns around in Larry's leather chair.

                    ED
          You may not know cars, but Larry here says
          he's willing to give you a shot at making
          a new ad for Checker.

                    JOHN
          Ed! I was just about to call you! Dinner
          was great last night.

                    LARRY
          We just signed an account...
               (Beat)
          ...a rather large account with Checker
          Moving Company. That is, only if you
          would do it.

                    JOHN
          Yeah! Of course I'll do it! I'll get
          started right away!

                    ED
          Great! Just keep your priorities straight
          and we'll get on fine.

INT. BOOK STORE - AFTERNOON

John walks through the aisles of a cavernous,
bookstore. He runs his finger along the spines,
browsing. Suddenly, a few feet down, one of the
books pops out and on to the floor. John looks
up, puzzled, as another book flies off the shelf.
John grins and quickly reaches through the stacks.

There's a shriek from the other side as he grabs a hand & pulls it through - it's Taylor. John holds her hand up to his mouth.

> JOHN
> You realize I'm going to have to punish you.

> TAYLOR
> No!

John makes as if to kiss her hand but licks it. Taylor squirms, giggling.

> TAYLOR (CONT'D)
> Aagh! That's disgusting!

Both are laughing now. John lets her hand go. John peaks through the stacks. Only Taylor's eyes are visible, but it's clear she's smiling hugely.

> JOHN
> Found what you're looking for?

Taylor looks deep into his eyes.

> TAYLOR
> Hell yes. Or, oh... You mean books.

> JOHN
> Books, yes.

> TAYLOR
> Almost. Give me ten minutes and we can go.

> JOHN
> No hurry, babe. Take your time.

Taylor blows a kiss through the stacks. John goes back to reading his book. We see he's looking at a book of modern art. The work is similar to the unfinished painting in his apartment.

Taylor's phone rings in the other aisle. She answers and starts talking quietly. John is oblivious, lost in thought staring at the painting on the page. Taylor's voice begins to rise. She's clearly upset.

> TAYLOR (O.S.)
> Mark?! What... Where are you? Mark, talk to me!

John snaps out of it and looks up.

> TAYLOR (CONT'D)
> Mark, please! You're not making sense!

John puts the book down and moves quickly to Taylor, who is starting to sound tearful.

> TAYLOR (CONT'D)
> No! Mark, don't! Please stay on! Talk to me!

JOHN'S P.O.V. rounds the corner and comes up behind Taylor.

She's completely distraught by now.

> TAYLOR (CONT'D)
> Goddamnit Mark, don't hang up! What do you want? Please, just tell me!

> JOHN
> What is it?

> TAYLOR
> It's my brother, he... Mark? Honey please don't do this. Please don't! Mark?
> (beat)
> Mark? Mark?!?!

Taylor falls to the ground, sobbing.

JOHN
Taylor, what the hell is going on?

Taylor manages to pull it together enough to talk.

TAYLOR
It's Mark... My little brother. He's... I don't know. He sounds like he was on something. And he's locked himself in a room and he's going to kill himself!

JOHN
You think it's just a cry for help, or something?

TAYLOR
No! I've never heard him like this! Something's seriously wrong. I think he means it this time!

JOHN
Where is he?

TAYLOR
I don't know. He got thrown out of his apartment. I think he was at someone's house.

JOHN
Whose house?

TAYLOR
I don't know! He didn't say!

John pulls out his cell phone and dials 911.

JOHN
Let me see your phone.

TAYLOR
What?!

                    JOHN
          Your phone. Let me see it.

Taylor hands him her phone. John starts going
through her call record while holding his phone up to
his ear.

                    JOHN (CONT'D)
          Yes, I'd like to report a suicide attempt.
          My girlfriend's brother just called her
          and said he's going to kill himself.
                    (beat)
          Just now, less than a minute ago.
                    (beat)
          Yes, ma'am, she says he sounded completely
          serious.

John looks at Taylor's phone.

                    JOHN (CONT'D)
          He called from 313-156-1723. It might be
          someone's house.
                    (beat)
          Yeah, I can hold.

John looks down at Taylor and smoothes her hair out
of her eyes.

                    JOHN (CONT'D)
          It'll be okay, babe.

          Taylor nods, wide-eyed.

John turns back to the phone.

                    JOHN (CONT'D)
          It is? Good. Can you...
                    (beat)
          Okay...
                    (beat)
          Okay. Can you...

                    (beat)
          Yes, you can reach me at this number.
          Thank you ma'am.

                         TAYLOR
          What happened?

                         JOHN
          Mark called from a residential number.
          They've got a police car right near there.
          She said they'll be there in minutes.
          She'll call us back when they know more.

Taylor latches onto John and breaks down.

INT. JOHN'S CAR -- NIGHT

John and Taylor are sitting in his car in the bookstore parking lot. Taylor is talking on the phone.

                         TAYLOR
          When can we see him?

Taylor listens for a bit, nodding.

                         TAYLOR (CONT'D)
          Thank you so much.

Taylor hangs up, still slightly tearful. John rubs her shoulder.

                         JOHN
          What's the story?

                         TAYLOR
          They got to him before he could...
                    (beat)
          He'll spend the night in jail, but they're
          probably just going to put him in rehab
          and counseling. But he's okay.

Taylor turns to John.

> TAYLOR (CONT'D)
> Thank you.

They embrace.

INT. JOHN'S APARTMENT - NIGHT

John is alone. He is working on the Checker account. A montage of John sitting at his desk tapping a pencil against his forehead. Throwing rolled up paper through a miniature basket ball hoop. Writing "I hate this" across an ad proposal. Laying on the floor with his feet on the couch. Looking at the corner of his painting behind the coach. Talking on the phone. Sifting though the couch cushions looking for change. Sitting on the couch, he looks at the remote, picks it up and turns on the TV.

INT. HALLWAY TO JOHN'S CUBICAL - MORNING

John is walking to his box When Larry sticks his head out of his office.

> LARRY
> How's our account going?

> JOHN
> Great! No problems!

INT. JOHN'S APARTMENT - NIGHT

John is on the telephone. His place is a mess.

> JOHN
> I'm sorry. I just can't do tonight.
> I'm so far behind.

> TAYLOR
> But I haven't seen you all week. When
> can I see you?

                    JOHN
Okay, here's what we'll do. I'll meet
you on tomorrow for dinner. How about at
Detroit Beer Company?

                    TAYLOR
Sounds good.

                    JOHN
Great! I gotta go now but I'll see you
then. Okay?

                    TAYLOR
Okay, bye hon.

INT. LARRY'S OFFICE - DAY

Larry is sitting in his mighty leather chair. John
is pacing in front of the huge desk.

                    LARRY
I don't know what your doing wrong but
Ed say's you need to get your priorities
strait. He says you're disappointing him.
Now I don't know what you did but stop
doing it! I want you to get out there and
bust your ass on this account!

                    JOHN
Yeah, okay Larry.

                    LARRY
Things are tight right now, John. This
account can either keep us afloat or sink
us strait to the bottom.

                    JOHN
Got it.

INT. JOHN'S APARTMENT - NIGHT

John walks through the door, tossing his keys on the

table. The telephone is ringing. John clumsily picks up the receiver balancing the bag in one hand.

JOHN
Hello?

TAYLOR
Where the hell are you?! I've been waiting for almost an hour.

JOHN
Taylor! Oh, Shit! I am so sorry My cell phone was turned off. I totally forgot. Oh, man.

TAYLOR
Well, get your ass over here!

JOHN
Uh, I really can't. I've got a lot to do. Your dad told Larry I was screwing up the account.

TAYLOR
What the hell! I already ordered wine! I can't just leave it.

JOHN
I'm really sorry. Why don't you just stay and have dinner.
    (Beat)
It's on me.

TAYLOR
You want me to eat alone?!

JOHN
Call a friend. Janice or something.

TAYLOR
Yeah, Janice or something.

                    JOHN
          I'm so sorry.

                    TAYLOR
          Well... Thanks for dinner.

                    JOHN
          I'll talk to you soon?

                    TAYLOR
          Talk to you later.

John hangs up the phone. John presses play on his
answering machine.

                    ED (O.S.)
          BEEP! Hey there, John I know you've been
          busting your hump on my account. It's
          making my girl a little lonely. Why don't
          you take the night off and go make her
          happy.

INT. DETROIT BEER COMPANY RESTAURANT - NIGHT

All sorts of different people are bustling around the
restaurant. John runs through the front door. He is
carrying some daisies. He scans the crowd and sees
Taylor eating at a distant table.

INT. TAYLOR'S TABLE - NIGHT

Taylor is eating a piece of chocolate pie. There is
a half eaten entree in front of the seat across from
her. John walks up to the table.

                    JOHN
          Hey, look who's here!

                    TAYLOR
          John! Uh, what are you doing here!?

                    JOHN

I decided that to take the night off.

CRAIG, Taylor's ex-boyfriend, walks up and grabs the chair across from Taylor.

                    TAYLOR
     Uh, John this is Craig.

                    CRAIG
     Good to meet you.

John is visibly pissed, but controls himself.

                    JOHN
     How are you? Enjoying dinner Craig?

                    TAYLOR
     John, let me...

                    JOHN
     I'll talk to you later.

John throws the flowers down on the table and storms off.

EXT. THE DETROIT BEER COMPANY - NIGHT

John stomps out the front door. Just as the doors finish closing behind him they open again and out comes Taylor.

                    TAYLOR
     John, wait!

                    JOHN
     Don't you have an ex-boyfriend you need to
     be attending to?

                    TAYLOR
     We just ran into each other. It's not
     like I called him.

                    JOHN
Sure, you just happened to run into your
ex-boyfriend five minutes after our big
fight?

                    TAYLOR
Would you let it go? I have something I
need to say to you.

He stops and faces her.

                    JOHN
What!?

                    TAYLOR
John, I miss you. I don't ever get to
see you. You're so wrapped up in that
damn account that you never have time
for me.

                    JOHN
That damned account is your father's.
It's making my career. It's really hard
work.

                    TAYLOR
So what! John look, if your going to
ignore me like this...

She starts to get teary eyed.

                    TAYLOR (CONT'D)
...then I really can't see you anymore.

                    JOHN
Fine! If that's what you want!

                    TAYLOR
That's not what I want. I want you! But
until you can focus on what's important
it's the way it will have to be.

                    JOHN
          Okay then. Thanks for clearing that up.

          John starts to walk away.

                    TAYLOR
          John, wait.

John stops and turns toward her again. Taylor is
outright crying now. She kisses her fore and ring
finger and places them on his lips. John stares at
her stonily. He turns away. As he walks away we see
him tearing up.

INT. JOHN'S CUBICAL - DAY

John sits at his desk doodling on a note pad and
looking very forlorn. Steve walks in and leans
against the desk.

                    STEVE
          How are you and Taylor?

                    JOHN
          Not so good.

                    STEVE
          Yeah, I know. I've been talking to
          Janice.

                    JOHN
          How are you guy's going?

                    STEVE
          Good. What's up with you and Taylor?

                    JOHN
          Well, last night she had a romantic dinner
          with her ex-boyfriend. On me.

                    STEVE
          Ouch!

JOHN
Yeah, I'm not too happy about it. What the hell was she thinkin'?

STEVE
You know, if I ever found a girl I thought was the one, I'd break up with her.

JOHN
There's that fear of commitment again.

STEVE
No, seriously. Think about it. When you dump a chick you see her at her worst. You know what she's like when she hates you. If you can make it through that, you're golden.

JOHN
You know, it's always like this. As soon as I start getting a girl broken in, you know, up to speed, something goes wrong. We watched all the required movies, listened to the required music, went to the required places. You know all the things you do with someone you want to understand you. Just as soon as we start to settle in -- we split up. I don't want to do that anymore! I want to fill the void once and for all. I don't think she ever loved me.

STEVE
So, it's over between you guys?

JOHN
I don't know. I think so. We said goodbye.

STEVE
This is probably the best thing for you if

you still have delusions about being some artsy fartsy painter. I mean, she would probably be kind of heavy on the upkeep - so, goodbye dreams.

                    JOHN
What do you mean?

                    STEVE
Think about it. She comes from rich folk. She has some pretty expensive tastes. You'd probably have to work your ass off to pay for the Williams Sanoma mixing bowls and shit.

John mulls this over.

                    STEVE (CONT'D)
I mean, she's unhappy if you work too much, but she'd probably be unhappy if you worked too little. You'd be walking a fine line for the rest of your days, man.

                    JOHN
I don't know. She might have been worth taking a chance on.

                    STEVE
Have you tried calling her?

                    JOHN
No.

                    STEVE
Are you gonna try?

                    JOHN
I don't know. I'm going to the folks house for dinner so it won't be tonight.

                    STEVE
Well, I guess I'll see you later tonight.

I gotta get back to work.

                    JOHN
          See ya.

INT. JOHN'S PARENTS HOUSE - NIGHT

John walks through the front door. On the wall going up the stairway are hundreds of framed photos of John and his family growing up over the years. John's MOM comes out of the kitchen wiping her hands on the apron.

                    MOM
          Oh, it is so good to see you. Just go on
          in your father and brother are waiting.
          Dinner will be ready in about a minute.

                    JOHN
          Hi mom.

INT. JOHN'S PARENTS DINNING ROOM - NIGHT

John's DAD and little sister are sitting at the table.

                    ALEX
          John! How you doing?

                    JOHN
          Oh, I've been better but I'm okay. Hey
          Dad.

                    DAD
          Hi John! Have a seat.

John takes his seat next to his brother.

He stares morosely at the place settings.

                    DAD (CONT'D)
          What's botherin' you son?

                    JOHN
          Oh, I bro...
               (beat)
          I got this big account at work and I'm
          getting nowhere. I hate it. I didn't
          like my job before but now I hate it.
          This is the least expressive I've ever
          been with my talents.

John's mom enters with a big bowl of salad.

                    DAD
          So what's the problem?

                    JOHN
          I'm just dry. I can't come up with a
          campaign to save my life. I'm the lead on
          this one.

                    DAD
          Wow! Your own project. That's great.

                    JOHN
          No, not great. If this doesn't work it's
          my ass on the line. Which may be a good
          thing.

                    DAD
          Well, everyone's got to work for someone.
          You can't like your job all the time.
          Who's the client?

                    JOHN
          Checker Moving Company, You know "The
          moving people"?

                    DAD
          Wow, I read about them in Cranes. That
          sounds pretty big.

                    JOHN

They want a complete overhaul. A new slogan, magazine layouts, and a commercial. I'm completely stuck.

                    ALEX
          At Checker Moving Company it's your move.

                    JOHN
          What did you say?

                    ALEX
          It's your move!

                    JOHN
          Oh my God! Alex that's brilliant!

John gets up and throws his napkin on the table.

                    JOHN (CONT'D)
          I got to go.

                    ALEX
          Stay off the drugs.

John slams the front door behind him.

EXT. JOHN'S PARENT'S HOUSE - NIGHT

John runs out the front door. Steve is next-door shooting hoops.

                    STEVE
          Where you goin?

                    JOHN
          I just had a break through. I'm going over to Ed's office to spring this on him.

                    STEVE
          Good luck.

Steve shoots and gets nothin' but net.

EXT. ED'S OFFICE - NIGHT

John opens the door and enters - He's met by BETTY, the receptionist, who's sitting behind the desk.

>BETTY
>Hi, can I help you?

>JOHN
>I need to see Ed, is he here?

>BETTY
>You're John? From the Ad Place?

>JOHN
>Yeah.

>BETTY
>His office is straight down the hall.

John rushed down the hall.

INT. ED'S OFFICE - NIGHT

John rushes through the front lobby as everyone else is leaving.

INT. ED'S OFFICE - NIGHT

Ed is sitting behind a big desk, writing.

>JOHN
>Knock knock.

>ED
>Ah, John, just the person I wanted to see. Come in.

>JOHN
>Ed, I just had a huge break through and I...

                    ED
          Now hold on kid. We need to have a talk.
          Have a seat.

John sits.

                    ED (CONT'D)
          Now, first off. Taylor told me about...
          you calling the cops on Mark.

                    JOHN
          I was just concerned. I thought he...

Ed waves him off.

                    ED
          Listen. You did the right thing. He's in
          rehab now, and they're going to put him in
          outpatient whatchamacallit...

                    JOHN
          Therapy.

Ed makes a face.

                    ED
          Therapy. Yeah. See, I kind of blame
          myself for some of Mark's troubles. I had
          to fire him when he started stealing from
          the company. I know he's his own man, but
          I just wasn't around when he was growing
          up. I... well, I was a pretty lousy dad.
          My priorities were all out of whack. You
          know?

John nods slowly.

                    ED (CONT'D)
          So this brings us to thing two. It has
          come to my attention that you can't keep
          your priorities strait. That you been
          putting business before your personal

life. More specifically, you don't know
that you need to love someone when they
love you. It's taken me a while to get
that right myself. But I got it. Now...
until you get your priorities strait I
can't have you working on this account.

                JOHN
I love Taylor too.

                ED
So, what are you doing here?

                JOHN
I don't know. I'll see you soon.

                ED
Yeah, call me tomorrow!

INT. HALLWAY TO TAYLOR'S APARTMENT - NIGHT

John is knocking like mad on Taylor's door.
Eventually Taylor opens the door.

                TAYLOR
Oh, hi John.

                JOHN
I want to get my priorities straight. Can
I come in?

Taylor hesitates.

                TAYLOR
Okay.

Taylor opens the door and lets him in.

INT. TAYLOR'S APARTMENT - NIGHT

The two walk in and sit on the couch.

TAYLOR
So, what's up?

JOHN
I am so sorry. I thought if I worked really hard on your father's account I would impress him and therefore impress you. I am so sorry. My mind is racing a million miles a second. I have so much I want to say to you. I didn't realize I was banishing you in favor of something that doesn't really matter.

TAYLOR
Slow down John, you're not making any sense. What are you saying?

JOHN
I'm saying that I put too much stock in that stupid account. I'm saying that I care for you so much.

TAYLOR
Hold on, that's my fathers account. It's important to him.

JOHN
Ok. I got that. It's not about your father. I just... I hate my job. I always have.

TAYLOR
Yeah, But you have to work John. I'm not going to go out with a bum.

JOHN
I know. I know. Ok. But what I'm saying is that I love you.

TAYLOR
You love me?

JOHN
Yes.

Long Pause (Possibly Pregnant).

TAYLOR
You can't love me.

JOHN
Why not?

TAYLOR
Because,
    (beat)
I love you.

JOHN
You do? But I loved you first.

TAYLOR
No way! That's impossible because I happen to know for a fact that I loved you first!

They start tickling each other.

JOHN
Let's move in together.

TAYLOR
What?!

JOHN
Yeah, I mean it. I've wanted you to for a long time. I just didn't think we were ready.

TAYLOR
You know what mister? Okay. Let's do it.

Taylor kisses her two fingers and places them on John's lips.

                    JOHN
          Pretty girl.

EXT. JOHN'S APARTMENT BUILDING - DAY

A giant Checkers Moving Van sits outside. Big burly men are

Moving out brown cardboard boxes. The front lawn is littered with random green furniture. The side of the van says "Checker Moving Company -- It's your move." John and Taylor are sitting on a sofa on the lawn. They are laughing and having a great time. Steve snaps a photo of them. Through clever editing the photo turns into a magazine ad for Checker Moving Company.

INT. HOUSE OF NINE - NIGHT

The night club is dark except for the narrow flashing lights. The music pounds. We find JOHN among the many Clubbers. John looks around the crowded club three girls catch his eye. TAYLOR Stands against a railing. She looks at her watch and looks around as if she were waiting for someone. LYDIA is sitting at a small table looking about hopefully. ZINN stands by the bar looking frustrated and unapproachable. She looks like the demon lover that every man fantasizes about being with at least once in their lives. John straitens his clothes and walks toward Lydia.

L.S.

John introduces himself and she seems very happy to meet him. She smiles. John takes the seat next to Lydia. An old friend of Lydia's approaches her -- HAND has two big scars on the palms of his hands. As Lydia and Hand speak unheard over the booming music a pleasant looking young girl named MONICA approaches John. She is smoking a cigarette.

                    MONICA
          Have you discovered the secret?

                    JOHN
          The secret to what?

                    MONICA
          The secret to talking to Lydia. Just
          smile and nod and you'll be okay.

As Monica departs she places a reassuring hand on
John's shoulder -- Lydia finishes with Hand.

                    LYDIA
          So...Where was I? Oh, yeah, twice today
          while I was eating I spilled food all
          over the place but none of it fell on me.
          I truly think there is some entity who
          follows me around and protects me from bad
          things.

John is smiling and nodding.

The sound shifts and becomes hollow -- it is obvious
to us that John is no longer paying attention to what
Lydia is saying.

                    LYDIA (CONT'D)
          You are so cool. I feel like I can talk
          to you about anything. You know I can
          tell you anything about me. I can tell
          you have a very open mind. Let me see
          your hand.

Lydia grabs John's hand, flips it over, and begins
reading his palm.

                    LYDIA (CONT'D)
          Ah. I see you are a very old soul. Like
          me. Do you want to go back to my place
          and talk?

John just smiles and nods.

INT. LYDIA'S BEDROOM - NIGHT

Lydia's room is done up in gauzy sheets hung from the ceiling -no hint of walls. There are pictures of angels and fairies are hung, taped, and glued all over the room. John is on top of Lydia deep in the throes of passion. Lydia's head keeps hitting the headboard. A piece of stray mosquito netting with crystals hung on the hem keeps smacking John in the forehead. He blows at the netting and tries to brush it away. Lydia looks up into John's eyes.

> LYDIA
> I want you to do it inside me.

> JOHN
> Huh?

> LYDIA
> Give me a piece of you. Cum inside me.

> JOHN
> Are you sure?

Lydia nods, looking very intense. John looks a bit disconcerted, but gives in and pumps furiously for a second before arching his back in ecstasy. He slumps to the bed beside her. All is quiet for a moment.

> LYDIA
> I want to tell you something and I want you to keep and open mind about it, okay? But that shouldn't be hard for you. You're so wonderful.

She turns to John and smiles. He smiles back nervously in anticipation of what she is going to tell him.

> LYDIA (CONT'D)

Okay, are you ready?
(Beat)
I am the Queen of the Faeries.

John finds an intense look of confusion on his face.

LYDIA (CONT'D)
I am the Queen of the Faeries. The faeries have chosen me to lead them. Do you believe in faeries John? I have this book...

Lydia reaches for a children's book called "Faeries" on a nearby shelf.

LYDIA (CONT'D)
You should borrow it. It is very enlightening.

JOHN
What does it mean -- being the... Queen of the Faeries?

LYDIA
I have certain powers. Like I can erase things from peoples minds if I concentrate on it.
(Beat)
I normally don't tell people about this but I truly feel for you. Uh, I can fly. I know this is hard to believe but it is true. All I need is more confidence in myself and I would be able to fly. I haven't tried it yet but I know if I had the confidence I could do it.

John sits up and puts his feet firmly on the floor.

JOHN
I need a drink of water.

He gets up and puts his pants on.

>   JOHN (CONT'D)
>   In fact, I think I'm gonna just head out.
>   I have to work in the morning.
>
>   LYDIA
>   Well...I though we were gonna cuddle for a
>   while! Is something wrong?
>
>   JOHN
>   No.
>
>   LYDIA
>   Then come back here for a while and lay
>   with me -- just for a minute. If we are
>   going to be together then we need to be
>   open with each other. Come here. Please.

With great reluctance John sits down on the edge of the bed refusing to take his feet off of the floor.

>   LYDIA (CONT'D)
>   Do you love me?
>
>   JOHN
>   What?!
>   (Beat)
>   I just met you. I hardly know you.
>
>   LYDIA
>   You mean after... but you could get to
>   know me.
>
>   JOHN
>   I need to get home.

John gets up and walks toward the door.

>   LYDIA
>   Well, don't forget the book.

John grabs the faerie book and leaves.

INT. JOHNS LIVING ROOM - NIGHT

John walks through his front door and tosses his keys into the golden tray. The answering machine on the small table next to the couch is blinking that he has a message. Pressing the button he takes off his jacket. Lydia's voice erupts from the machine.

                    LYDIA (O.S.)
          BEEP! Hi John this is Lydia. I just
          wanted to say to you that I had a really
          good time with you tonight and that if you
          ever do anything to piss me off I will
          cast a spell on you. You would be fuckin'
          dead. Anyway, sweet dreams to you. I
          love you.

John looks concerned.

INT. JOHN'S OFFICE ELEVATOR - MORNING

John is standing in the back of the lift with two other gentleman and a lady. The doors begin to close but before they can a briefcase slams into crack, re-opening the doors. In walks Steve, who is winded from running, takes his place next to John.

                    STEVE
          Hey buddy, what's going on?

                    JOHN
          Do you remember that kind of psycho girl
          you met a few months ago?

                    STEVE
          Yeah, I still have nightmares.

                    JOHN
          Last night I met this chick. I thought

she was cool and everything was going okay. That's when she declared her love for me and told me she would cast a spell on me if I ever...
(beat)
...made her mad.

               STEVE
There's nothing like meeting a batshit insane girl to make you stop talking to women you don't know.
(singing)
She keeps calling me...

               JOHN
Shut up. STEVE (singing louder) Nailed my cat to a treeeeeee!

INT. JOHN'S APARTMENT - EARLY EVENING

The door to John's apartment opens and he steps through. Tossing his keys onto the table by the door he presses play on the answering machine which has a bright red light flashing intensely.

LYDIA (O.S.)
    BEEP! Hi John, Just thought I would call and say hello.
        (beat)
    BEEP! Hey there my sweet, just calling to say hey -- where are you?
        (beat)
    BEEP! John, this is Lydia. Where are you? Hey, it's Friday. We should get together. Call me. Bye.
        (beat)
    BEEP! Why the fuck haven't you called me! I really want to see you.
        (beat)
    BEEP! You bastard! Call me! Or fuck you!

                    (beat)
          BEEP! John, I think I'm pregnant. Call
          me.

John hits the stop button with all of his might just
as the next "beep" sounds. He flips the down button
on his Caller ID. Thirty three calls from Lydia, all
within fifteen minutes of each other.

INT. THOMAS VIDEO - NIGHT

John and Steve walk down separate row's. Steve in
the Suspense section looking for a flick, John in the
Romance.

                    STEVE
          Hey, how about this one. Fatal
          Attraction!

                    JOHN
          Put that back you ass! Was that really
          not that funny when I did it to you?

John bumps into Monica. Monica acts like they're old
friends.

                    MONICA
          Hey! How are you?

                    JOHN
          Oh, hi. Good, how are you?

                    MONICA
          Hey, How's Lydia?

                    JOHN
          Oh my God! What a psycho! She keeps
          calling me!

                    MONICA
          Has she cast a spell on you yet?

JOHN
Probably.

MONICA
Yeah, she'll do that to you. I pissed her off when I was dating her a few months ago...

In the background we see Steve's head snap up at the mention of girl on girl action.

MONICA (CONT'D)
She cast a spell on me.

Steve appears next to Monica.

STEVE
Hi.

JOHN
Oh, hey this is my friend Steve. Steve -- uh, what's your name?

MONICA
Monica. She shakes Steve's hand.

MONICA (CONT'D)
(To John)
And you are?

JOHN
John.

MONICA
What movie are you guys here for?

STEVE
We don't know.

MONICA
Oh, you're the browsing type? I don't understand that. I always know exactly

what I want.

She looks into John's eyes.

> MONICA (CONT'D)
> For example, I'm here to get the new Holiday Martin movie. Have you met her?

John shakes his head.

> MONICA (CONT'D)
> Her parties are great. I think her movies are somewhat sophomoric but fun. I don't know - she's kind of like the Andy Warhol of Detroit.

John and Steve nod knowingly.

> MONICA (CONT'D)
> Speaking of parties, I'm having a get together later tonight. Why don't you guys stop by?

Monica hands him a card.

> MONICA (CONT'D)
> Give me a call in few hours.

Monica smiles and walks away. John and Steve look at each other and shake their heads to the side as if to say "what the hell?"

INT. HALLWAY, MONICA'S APARTMENT BUILDING - NIGHT

John and Steve are standing outside Monica's door. They knock. Monica yells from inside.

> MONICA (O.S.)
> It's open!

INT. MONICA'S APARTMENT - NIGHT

Steve and John walk in. METHANIE and Monica are sitting on the floor. A lit cigarette sits in the ashtray in front of them.

> METHANIE
> (In mid sentence.)
> ...and then Mark completely crapped out - he wouldn't lend Brian any more cash and kicked us all out of his place. Which really pissed off Brian. Zinn wanted to come back here to get loaded, but we nixxed that idea - I know how you feel about doing that here.

> MONICA
> She's such a total bitch! Brian only lets her hang around because she's the only girl as crazy as he is. They're like the underground answer to Bonnie and Clyde. If he ever brings her back here wasted he's out on the street. I'll find someone else to pay half the rent.

John and Steve sit down on the couch.

> JOHN
> Hey. Monica grins up at him.

> MONICA
> Hey yourself. Natalie, this is John and Steve.

The three exchange greetings.

> MONICA (CONT'D)
> Hey Nat, what's Shawn doing tonight?

> METHANIE
> Oh, Friday is his band night. They're rehearsing.

                    MONICA
          Where's the kid?

                    METHANIE
          I gave him to the folks tonight so I could
          "indulge" with Brian.

Monica shorts derisively.

                    MONICA
          Maybe if indulged a whole bunch I could
          live with Zinn for a night. Well,
          probably not. Do you guys ever partake?

Steve And John shake their heads "no".

                    JOHN
          I don't know, I guess I would try anything
          once.

                    STEVE
          That stuff scares the shit out of me.

                    MONICA
          Don't let the public service announcements
          fool you. It's not that bad. In fact, it
          can be very good.

She smiles seductively.

                    METHANIE
          Hey, are we gonna watch this movie or
          what? I have to pick up the kid before
          one.

INT. MONICA'S APARTMENT - NIGHT

The movie is now half over and the room is shrouded
in smoke. The lights are out and the whole gang
is really into the movie. On the TV the telephone
rings. Right after the telephone in Monica's
apartment rings. Monica gets up to answer it and

checks her caller ID.

                    MONICA
    It's Lydia! What the hell is...

She picks up the phone.

                MONICA (CONT'D)
    Hello?

A muffled voice can be heard on the other end of the line.

Monica cups her hand over the receiver and whispers to John.

                MONICA (CONT'D)
    She's looking for you! John desperately gives the signal that he's not there.

Monica takes her hand away from the receiver.

                MONICA (CONT'D)
    Umm, Lydia. What's going on?
        (beat)
    Who's this John guy? Why the hell would he be here?

A muffled voice can be heard offering a response and continues.

                MONICA (CONT'D)
    Uh huh, okay, umm, alright then.
        (beat)
    Yes, okay good enough, umm, yeah, good night.
        (beat)
    Bye now.

Monica hangs up the phone with the muffled voice still talking and walks back to her seat on the couch. She lights a cigarette and looks at John.

                    MONICA (CONT'D)
          She wanted to know if you were here. I
          wondered how the hell she knew you were
          here and I thought that maybe she was
          just doing the classic stalker thing and
          followed you. But no, she's just calling
          everyone she knows to see if you're with
          them.

                    STEVE
          What are the chances?

                    METHANIE
          Wow, what a psycho bitch! Man, you got
          a long road in front of you too! She
          doesn't give up very easy. You should
          just pack up and move to another city.

Some of the other party goers snicker.

                    JOHN
          This is getting a little out of hand. I'm
          a little afraid to go home tonight.

                                        DISSOLVE TO:

INT. MONICA'S APARTMENT - NIGHT

The Martin flick is ending. The lights come on and
everyone starts filtering out. Monica leans over to
John.

                    MONICA
          You know if you're still scared to go home
          -- you could just stay here tonight.

                    JOHN
          Hmmm, what a tempting offer.
               (Beat)
          Okay, I'm easy.

                    MONICA

Well, this way you don't have to face the
thousand or so calls on your machine when
you get home.

                  JOHN
Of course.

John walks over to Steve who is putting on his sport coat.

                  JOHN (CONT'D)
Listen, I have been invited to stay the
night.

                  STEVE
Well, alright! You have a good time.
Natalie wants to go get some coffee.

Methanie walks up to the boys.

                  METHANIE
You ready Stevo?

                  STEVE
See ya my man!

The two friends shake hands and Steve leaves with the crowd out the door leaving John and Monica alone. Monica is taking a few glasses to the kitchen.

INT. MONICA'S KITCHEN - NIGHT

John Follows Monica in through the door, Monica deposits her glasses into the sink.

                  JOHN
So, the old why don't you stay the night
so you don't have to face the wrath of the
Queen of the Faeries ploy, huh?

                  MONICA
Saw right through it, huh?

She wipes her hands off on her pants and then slowly wraps them around John's waist. They kiss, tentatively at first then with growing intensity. John pushes Monica against the wall and they go at each other in earnest. Monica pulls back for a moment and looks over John's shoulder.

> MONICA (CONT'D)
> Kitchen table's closer than the bed.

John smiles. They bolt out of frame. Fade to black amidst sounds of crazed sex.

INT. ELEVATOR AT JOHN'S OFFICE - MORNING

John stands in the back holding his briefcase in front of him casually. The doors begin to close but are re-opened by Steve's briefcase. Steve enters the elevator. The doors close and the elevator begins to move.

> STEVE
> So, how's your girlfriend?

> JOHN
> Which one?

> STEVE
> You salty sea dog!

> JOHN
> No, Lydia called me thirty six times over the weekend. But...I did spend

> JOHN (CONT'D)
> most of Saturday with Monica. We just mucked around her place. I wanted to see her again yesterday but she was out all day, so I left a message.

> STEVE
> Oh. Hey, Natalie called yesterday and

invited us to go to the club on Tuesday night.

                    JOHN
          Cool, that sounds good.

The elevator doors open.

INT. JOHN'S CUBICAL - DAY

John is on the Phone with Monica's machine.

                    JOHN
          Oh, hey Monica this is John again. Just
          calling to say hey. Uh, I guess I'll see
          you tonight at the club. Talk to you.

INT. THE HOUSE OF NINE - NIGHT

John and Steve walk in and wade they're way through the thick crowd. They look lost. Soon, however, they see Methanie dancing and approach her.

                    METHANIE
          Hey, guys. How are you? Oh hey...

She grabs SHAWN who is talking to someone and drags him over.

                    METHANIE (CONT'D)
          ...this is my man, Shawn. They all shake
          hands.

                    SHAWN
          Glad to meet ya.

Suddenly Mark, a lanky, nervous looking man brushes past him, making a beeline for Methanie. Shawn turns to watch him.

                    SHAWN (CONT'D)
          Uh, hi Mark.

Mark stops in front of Methanie. Methanie is guarded, arms crossed, but listens as he starts talking at her. Shawn turns back to John.

                    SHAWN (CONT'D)
          So, how's your problem with our Lydia?

Behind Shawn we see Mark gesturing wildly, obviously upset. Methanie shrugs helplessly.

                    JOHN
          Brother, you don't know the half of it.

                    SHAWN
          How long has this been going on?

                    JOHN
          Just a few days now.

In the background Mark stalks off angrily. Methanie watches him go.

                    SHAWN (LAUGHING)
          Man, are you in for a treat! So what do you guys do for a living?

                    JOHN
          We're both in advertising -- McMann

                    SHAWN
          What time do you have to get up in the morning?

                    JOHN
          I don't know. Around six usually.

                    SHAWN
          I have a little theory about that. The work day and early mornings are a way for the government to keep you all in line.

John and Steve laugh politely, thinking he's kidding.

Their smiles freeze as they realize Shawn is totally serious.

>   JOHN
> Uh....

>   SHAWN
> See, most of us are so trained to wake
> up artificially, you know, like by alarm
> clocks and stuff, that by the end of the
> day no one has the ambition or energy to
> do anything else even remotely productive.
> But if we were allowed to wake up when
> we naturally woke up we would be more
> productive and aware. And we were more
> productive and aware, we might be more
> inspired to revolt or something!

There is a stunned pause from John and Steve.

>   STEVE
> You know... oddly enough that thought had
> never entered my mind. Ever.

Shawn grins and bops off to see someone else. John notices Monica dancing a little way through the crowd and makes his way toward her.

>   JOHN
> Hey there. How are you?

>   MONICA
> Oh. Hey John.

>   JOHN
> I tried calling. I left messages. Why
> haven't you called back?

>   MONICA
> You know, I've been really busy. Sorry.

>   JOHN

When I got home from your place Lydia had called me twenty times. She called thirty six times over the weekend and twelve times yesterday and today. Pretty crazy huh?

Monica gives John a courtesy laugh and continues to dance. John looks snubbed.

INT. THE HOUSE OF NINE - NIGHT

MONTAGE:

John hangs out at the bar by himself feeling ignored by Monica. Methanie and Steve dance. Shawn talks to a guy. Monica finally grabs John from the bar - she and John dance to a heavy but slower song toward the end of the night showing she hasn't forgotten him after all.

EXT. PARKING LOT OF THE CITY - NIGHT

It is a cool evening. Their breath can be seen when they speak. The gang is all leaving together.

          JOHN
Well, guys. It has been a good night.

          STEVE
Yeah, no doubt about it.

          SHAWN
It was really good meeting you guys. You should come over sometime. You can meet the kid.

          STEVE
That sounds great.

          JOHN
Yeah.

They begin to split for their respective cars.

Methanie and Steve give a quick hug. Monica grabs John and they kiss.

> JOHN
> You know, I could fall for you.

Monica smiles and walks away toward her car.

INT. HALLWAY OF JOHN'S APARTMENT BUILDING - NIGHT

John is walking down the dimly lit passage while fishing for his keys in his pocket. On the floor in front of his door is a can of Coke with a rosary wrapped around it. He looks concerned as he opens his door. He steps through careful not to touch the unusual shrine outside his door.

INT. JOHN'S APARTMENT - NIGHT

He looks at the machine and sees that the "you have a message" light is blinking. John sighs.

> JOHN
> Time to check Lydia. He presses the button.

He flips through his mail as she speaks.

> LYDIA (O.S.)
> BEEP! Hi, hon. Just called to say hi. Welcome home.

John hams it up, talking back to the machine.

> JOHN
> Thanks honey! How are you? Still crazy?

> LYDIA (O.S.)
> BEEP! You know. I'm trying to be nice to you... but why won't you call me back?

JOHN
Because you're completely insane!

LYDIA (O.S.)
BEEP! I saw you tonight. With Monica. You know, that really sucks. You suck. I hate your fuckin' guts!

JOHN
Good then stop calling me.

LYDIA (O.S.)
BEEP! Well, I guess your not gonna call me again. Good night.

INT. JOHN'S CUBICAL - DAY

John is on the telephone, once again with Monica's machine.

JOHN
Monica, John. Just calling to see if you want to do something soon. Talk to you bye.

He hangs up the phone -- sighing loudly. Steve pops his head over the side of the cubical like a gopher.

STEVE
What's up?

JOHN
So, I get home last night to find a little present for me.

STEVE
From...?

JOHN
You guessed it. She left me a Coke Can with a rosary wrapped around it. What the heck is that all about?

                    STEVE
          So, what did you do with it?

                    JOHN
          Huh? Well, I left it out all night but I
          brought it in this morning.

                    STEVE
          Did you drink the Coke at least?

                    JOHN
          Wh... no! She probably cursed it or
          something.

                    STEVE
          Nat was telling me she and Shawn used
          to be good friends with Lydia. Well,
          they had a similar experience with her.
          They say there's like these steps that
          you'll go through with her but she will
          eventually quit.

                    JOHN
          How long did it take for them?

                    STEVE
          Something like thirteen months. You
          should go talk to them. They probably
          have some good insight into the
          situation. Shawn's pretty cool once you
          get past the conspiracy stuff.

INT. METHANIE AND SHAWN'S PLACE - EARLY EVENING

Their apartment has toys scattered across the floor
and is decorated with salvation army furniture.
Shawn is watching TV and gluing pennies to his combat
boots. Steve is sitting next to him.

INT. METHANIE AND SHAWN'S KITCHEN -- EARLY EVENING

John is talking to Methanie while she feeds her baby in the high chair. A cigarette dangles from her lips.

                METHANIE
Why don't you call Lydia and tell her to lay off?

                JOHN
Yeah, I could give it a try. I don't think it will help though. Did it do anything for you?

                METHANIE
Not a thing. Has she started leaving things outside you door?

                JOHN
Yeah, a pop can and a rosary. What is that supposed to mean?

                METHANIE
With Lydia, who knows. Start to expect things in the mail box and by your Car too. It's almost like she has nothing better to do then harass people.

                JOHN
Doesn't she have a job?

                METHANIE
She did when Shawn and I dated her. She was a physician's assistant.

                JOHN
So, What's up with Monica?

                METHANIE
What do you mean?

                JOHN
Well, it's like I call her to see if she

wants to do something and she never calls me back.

> **METHANIE**
> Well, she has been really busy lately. You should cool down a bit though. She's the type of gal who likes her space.

> **JOHN**
> Hmmm?

> **METHANIE**
> I mean, you don't like Lydia calling you all the time. I know this isn't even remotely the same level but...

> **JOHN**
> It is similar.

> **METHANIE**
> Hell, she'd probably call you if you just gave her time to digest how much she likes you.

> **JOHN**
> So I should stop calling her?

> **METHANIE**
> No, just meter your calls. If you left a message yesterday don't call until Wednesday. Give her a chance to miss you.

The feeding being done Methanie picks up her child, cigarette still in her mouth, and walks toward the living room. Smoke is getting all over the child's face.

> **METHANIE (CONT'D)**
> Monica does like you. I've seen her with lots of people. She definitely likes you more than most.

INT. JOHN'S BEDROOM - NIGHT

John is holding the telephone receiver in his hand. The phone is ringing. It is answered on the other end.

                JOHN
    Hello, Lydia? Hey, this is John.

The muffled voice on the other end of the line sounds very excited.

                JOHN (CONT'D)
    Hold on Lydia. I am calling you to tell
    you, you have got to stop calling me.

The muffled voice sounds really angry as Lydia lays it into John.

                JOHN (CONT'D)
    Yes, yes I know you're going to cast a
    spell on me. Actually I thought that
    maybe you already did.

More angry muffled voice.

                JOHN (CONT'D)
    Look Lydia, I understand but I have to go.
    Good bye.

There is a muffled slam on the other end as Lydia hangs up the phone. John hangs up his phone.

EXT. JOHN'S APARTMENT BUILDING - MORNING

John steps out onto the street to see his car has a bouquet of dead flowers on the hood of his car where the heart would be (If a car had one - Dig?) He stops about ten feet from his car and just looks at it. A soft breeze kicks up and whisks the petals away.

INT. JOHN'S CUBICAL - DAY

John is seated at his desk. He leans back in his swivel chair. He is deep in thought. He is crushing a dead flower petal between his thumb and forefinger. The telephone rings and John picks up the receiver.

     JOHN
John.

     MONICA (O.S.)
Hey, this is Monica.

John drops the flower to the floor and smiles.

     JOHN
Monica, how are you?

     MONICA
Good. Hey where have you been? I've missed getting your calls.

     JOHN
Well, you know, I've been busy.

     MONICA
Well, are you busy for lunch?

     JOHN
  (Looking at his planner.)
Well, I could probably squeeze you in.

     MONICA
Ha! You bastard! Did you like the Holiday Martin film?

     JOHN
Yeah, it was sexy.

     MONICA
She just opened an exhibit at the Tangent

Gallery. Meet me there at twelve thirty.

              JOHN
The Tangent Gallery huh? Yeah, okay. See you then.

John hangs up the phone. He has a big smile on his face.

INT. THE TANGENT GALLERY - DAY

The gallery is bustling. John scans the crowd but cannot see Monica anywhere.

              MONICA
John, over here!

She waves at him. Monica is dressed professionally in a dark suit. John didn't recognize her.

              JOHN
Monica! You look...wow!

              MONICA
Yeah, the secret daytime life of Monica.

              JOHN
You look great.

They stop in front of a painting, a self portrait of Holiday Martin. They study it for a moment.

              JOHN (CONT'D)
She's good.

              MONICA
Very.

              JOHN
Oils are a bitch to work with.

John gestures at the painting.

JOHN (CONT'D)
But if you want this built-up, sculptural feel there's nothing better. Acrylics can sort of pull it off, but they don't have the luster you get with oils.

MONICA
They teach you that in advertising school?

JOHN
No, I... I used to paint a lot, before I started doing the day job thing.

MONICA
Why'd you stop?

JOHN
Not enough time, I guess. But I miss it. It gave me... life.

MONICA
Then you never should have stopped. Life is an act of creation. As soon as you stop doing what you love you die.

John stares at the painting intently.

JOHN
Yeah, that sounds about right...

John looks uncomfortable. In an effort to change the subject he moves to look at a painting of a somewhat tarnished but impressive art Deco office building soaring above a gnarly looking burnt out building in one of Detroit's rougher areas.

JOHN (CONT'D)
You gotta wonder what happened.

Monica moves up beside the painting.

MONICA
How do you mean?

JOHN
To this city. You've got this vital metropolis and then... it withered on the vine. It's nothing but husks barely hanging on.

MONICA
Detroit isn't dead, it's just lost.

JOHN
You think so?

MONICA
Absolutely. Cities are people. And people can endure much worse than just forgetting who they are. When enough people wake up it'll be back.

Monica looks pointedly at John, smiling and moves on to another painting. John looks up at the two buildings for a moment before following her.

MONICA (CONT'D)
Hey, would you like to try something really fun?

JOHN
I'm always up for fun.

MONICA
Brian says our "friend" has some good stuff in. You up for it?

John hesitates for beat and then nods.

JOHN
Yeah, why not?

MONICA

I'll call you soon. We'll have fun.

>Monica kisses John, and they go their separate ways.

INT. JOHN'S CAR - DAY

Tall buildings loom above the cement square as John and Steve drive down the street.

>STEVE
>So you called her and told the bitch to step off?

>JOHN
>Yeah, I don't think she took it very well. I just want to get up and go to work everyday. I don't need any excitement.

>STEVE
>Well, I guess Nat and Shawn are having a get together at their place. You could drown your sorrows in a big tall glass of Monica.

John grins like a schoolboy.

>JOHN
>That is the best idea I've heard all week.

>STEVE
>Can I get an amen?

>JOHN
>Amen.

INT. LOBBY OF METHANIE AND SHAWN'S APARTMENT BUILDING - DAY

John walks through the glass doors and see's a young girl kissing her mother goodbye. She grabs her little backpack and runs out the door to a man who is waiting outside on the sidewalk.

INT. SHAWN AND METHANIE'S APARTMENT STAIRWELL - DAY

John is ascending the stairs. Shawn comes out and waves John up from the landing.

                SHAWN
John - come on up.

                JOHN
I've been here - I know where I'm going.

INT. SHAWN AND METHANIE'S APARTMENT - DAY

John opens the door and looks into the apartment. There is a load of amps and other equipment set up in the living room. Shawn stands in the middle of the mess, fiddling around with a guitar.

                JOHN
Hey.

                SHAWN
What's up?

                JOHN
So where's Nat?

                SHAWN
They're putting the *fun* back in funeral.

                JOHN
Wow... Who, um....

                SHAWN
               (SHRUGS)
I don't think it was anyone you knew. You didn't need to know him.

                    JOHN (CONT'D)
          So he wasn't on your list of drinking
          buddies?

                    SHAWN
          You could say that.

There's a moment of awkward silence.

                    SHAWN (CONT'D)
          They're not going to be home until a lot
          later.

                    JOHN
          Ok. I guess I'll see them soon.

                    SHAWN
          See you man.

INT. JOHN'S APARTMENT BUILDING HALLWAY - EVENING

John walks toward his door. Taped to the door is a
long strand of hair that could only belong to Lydia.

INT. JOHN'S APARTMENT - NIGHT

John throws his keys on the table and looks toward
the machine. There is only one message. John
presses play.

                    LYDIA (O.S.)
          BEEP! Oh, uh hi John this is Lydia.
          I'm just calling to say hello. Last
          time we spoke you said that you would
          talk to me. I was just calling to say
          hi.

At that moment the telephone rings. John walks
toward the kitchen, opting to let the machine get it.

                    JOHN (O.S.)
               (voice on the machine)

>   Hello, this is John, I can't come to the
>   phone, leave a message.
>
>   MOM
>   BEEP! Oh, my God John it's terrible! In
>   our home! If you're there pick up the
>   phone!

John runs out of the Kitchen and grabs the phone.

>   JOHN
>   Mom, mom. What's up?

A hysterical muffled voice can be heard through the receiver.

>   JOHN (CONT'D)
>   They took what? Okay, I'm coming right
>   over.

EXT. JOHN'S PARENTS HOUSE - NIGHT

An unmarked car sits in the driveway. John opens the front door and enters.

INT. JOHN'S PARENTS HOUSE - NIGHT

John instantly notices that all of the photos of him that line the wall of the stairway are gone. The frames are still there, only the photos of him are gone. The pictures of his sister and other relatives are all intact.

INT. JOHN'S PARENT'S LIVING ROOM - NIGHT

John's parent's along with Alex, sit on the couch while Detective Marx interrogates them. John enters the room.

>   DETECTIVE MARX
>   ...so you have no idea who...

                    MOM
John, my baby! Who would do something
like this?

                    JOHN
Hey mom, Dad.

                    DAD
John. This is detective Marx. Detective,
this is our son John.

Detective Marx and John shake hands.

                    JOHN
It's a pleasure to meet you sir.

                    DETECTIVE MARX
Likewise. We were just discussing
who might have done this. They seem
especially interested in you. Do you know
who might be behind this?

                    JOHN
Well, I met a girl a few weeks ago. She's
kind of stalking me.

                    DETECTIVE MARX
Can you elaborate on that at all?

                    JOHN
Well, I think she did it.

                    DETECTIVE MARX
Why?

                    JOHN
Well, like I said she has been stalking
me.

                    DETECTIVE MARX
What does that mean?

                    JOHN
          You know, stalking. Following me around.
          Leaving things outside my door. Covering
          my car in rose petals.

                    DETECTIVE MARX
          What is your relationship with this girl?

                    JOHN
          I met her at a club.

                    DETECTIVE MARX
          I see. How many times have you seen her?

                    JOHN
          Only once.

                    DETECTIVE MARX
          Only once?! Why is she so obsessed with
          you?

                    JOHN
          She's crazy -- I don't know.

                    DETECTIVE MARX
          What did you do when you met her?

John looks uncomfortably at his mother who is
molesting a string of rosary beads. Alex snickers --
he knows what they did.

                    JOHN
          You know, stuff.

                    DETECTIVE MARX
          No, I really don't know. Why don't you
          tell me?

                    JOHN
          Look I met a girl and we spent some time
          together, okay?

                    DETECTIVE MARX
          I see. What was this girl's last name?

                    JOHN
          I don't know.

                    MARX
          I see. Do you know where she lives?

                    JOHN
          I don't remember.

                    DETECTIVE MARX
          I see.

                                        DISSOLVE TO:

INT. JOHN'S PARENT'S HOUSE - NIGHT

John is putting on his jacket. Mom, Dad, and Alex
are waiting to say goodbye. John hugs his mother.

                    JOHN
          Everything will be alright.

He kisses her on the cheek.

                    MOM
          I know it.

                    DAD
          Well keep in touch.

                    ALEX
          Wear a condom!

                    MOM
          Alex!

EXT. JOHN'S PARENTS HOUSE - NIGHT

John walks out onto the lawn toward his car. Dad

closes the door. Standing by John's Auto is Steve, wearing only sweatpants, a T-shirt, and slippers. He is eating a King Don.

                    STEVE
          What happened?

                    JOHN
          Why didn't you come over?

                    STEVE
          Myth Busters was on. So what's up?

                    JOHN
          Lydia struck again.

                    STEVE
          Here?

                    JOHN
          Yeah, the crazy bitch took all of my childhood pictures.

                    STEVE
          Wacky.

                    JOHN
          Yeah.

                    STEVE
          Well she needs ' 91em for the altar.

                    JOHN
          You prick! Steve laughs.

                    JOHN (CONT'D)
          That cop was a real cock master. He wanted me to say that I greased Lydia up and did her like a big boy in front of my mother.

                    STEVE

That just ain't right.

              JOHN
    I got to go. I have a huge headache.

INT. MONICA AND BRIAN'S APARTMENT - NIGHT

Monica sits at the table covered in papers and her laptop, talking on the phone.

              MONICA
    From your parents' house?!

INT. JOHN'S CAR - NIGHT

John is driving and talking on his cellphone.

              JOHN
    Every last one. Even the pictures where I
    was, like two.

INT. MONICA AND BRIAN'S APARTMENT - NIGHT

              MONICA
    Wow. Well, you are mighty fine in the
    sack. I can see why she'd obsess.

INT. JOHN'S CAR - NIGHT

              JOHN
    You are too kind. Listen, I could use
    some distraction from this. You up for a
    late dinner?

INT. MONICA AND BRIAN'S APARTMENT - NIGHT

Behind Monica we see Brian and Zinn heading out for the evening.

              MONICA
    Not tonight, sweety. I really want to get
    some work done. Can I get a raincheck?

                    Tomorrow at the club?

INT. JOHN'S CAR - NIGHT

                         JOHN
                    You've got a deal.

                         MONICA (O.S.)
                    Why don't you go home and find something
                    to keep your mind off it.

                         JOHN
                    Will do. See you tomorrow.

                         MONICA (O.S.)
                    Nighty, night sweety.

INT. JOHN'S APARTMENT - NIGHT

John comes in and throws his keys on the table. He
plops down in front of the TV and switches it on,
looking at it without watching. After a moment
he switches it back off. John gets up and starts
pacing. Something catches his eye. It's his
painting, just a corner peaking out from behind the
couch. He walks over and pulls it out, then reaches
down behind the couch and pulls out an easel. John
sets the painting up and sits down, staring at it.
Suddenly there's a knock at the door. John ignores
it, but whoever it is knocks again, louder.

John gets up and looks out the peep hole. There's
nobody there. He opens the door and looks around.
Nothing. As he's closing the door he sees a small
envelope taped to the door. He opens it and spills
out its contents; long finger nails and rose petals.
John looks around nervously and ducks back inside.

INT. THE HOUSE OF NINE - NIGHT

John and Steve make a B-line through the crowd for
the usual corner. All of the familiar faces are

there. Shawn is waving his hands in front of his face, walking along with them as they make their way through the crowd.

                    SHAWN
          Hey! Man, I gotta tell you guys some
          shit. Back in the sixties the government
          secretly started up the counterculture
          that taught us that conformity and being
          a follower is bad. You know, question
          authority. This was all a plot to make
          impossible for us -- common man --to
          revolt Because no one would follow any
          leader or authority figure. You know,
          everyone's a chief and there's no Indians.
          It's total social chaos, man. It blew
          up in their faces though! It became
          impossible for the cops to keep order
          since nobody listened to them anymore.
          I'm having a great time, man!

Monica comes over and gives John a big wet kiss.

                    MONICA
          Hey lover!

                    JOHN
          Hey! What the hell is Shawn going on
          about?

                    MONICA
          I have no idea. He's been indulging.

                    JOHN
          Maybe I'll understand him more after I try
          it.

                    MONICA
          You ready?

                    JOHN

Yeah! If you can handle it then...

He is interrupted by BRIAN. He pushes John aside with his shoulder and hugs Monica. Brian's presence is very self assured and powerful. John notices Zinn, dressed in sexy leathers and lace, standing by the bar waiting for Brian.

> MONICA
> Brian, this is John. John, my roommate Brian.

> BRIAN
> How are you?

> JOHN
> Good...

> BRIAN
> (To Monica.)
> I gotta go, Zinn's buggin' the shit out of me.

Brian walks over to Zinn who kisses him deeply and makes sure Monica sees it. They move away toward the bar. Monica watches him go.

> MONICA
> What a dick.

John notices Hand walk up to Brian and Zinn. Hand shakes Zinn's hand with both of his. John see's that on both side of each hand is a scare right in the middle of his palms.

> JOHN
> I've seen that guy before.

> MONICA
> That's Hand. One day he just showed up. He can be a bit uppity but he's really well connected. If you're with him you

can get anywhere in this city.

                    JOHN
          What's up with his hands?

                    MONICA
          Rumor has it there's this chick lurking
          in the city who takes people she deems
          "worthy" and nails them to the floor like
          Jesus Christ and fucks 'em silly. I guess
          it's the only way she gets off. There are
          only a few more like him out there.

                    JOHN
          That's crazy.
               (Beat)
          It's probably Lydia.

                    MONICA
          No shit.

INT. JOHN'S APARTMENT - NIGHT

John comes home from the Club and throws his keys
down as usual. He checks the Machine and is relieved
to see that there are no messages. He walks toward
his bathroom.

INT. JOHN'S BATHROOM - NIGHT

John opens the medicine chest and grabs the extra
strength aspirin bottle. He starts to open it when
he notices a small black velvet bag sitting on the
little glass shelf. He stares at the bag, afraid to
touch it. Finally he grabs the bag and pulls open
the drawstrings. Inside he finds two small vials.
One is filled with blood. The other is filled with a
clear liquid and is marked "Tears."

INT. JOHN'S APARTMENT - NIGHT

John has changed into some sweatpants and a T-shirt.

He is escorting Detective Marx to the door.

                    DETECTIVE MARX
          Well, she's persistent. I'll give her
          that. We'll contact your friends and
          see if any of them know where she lives.
          We'll get this thing taken care of.

                    JOHN
          Thanks officer, have a good night.

John closes the door and locks it. He walks over to his couch and sits.

EXT. STREET OUTSIDE JOHN'S PLACE - DAY

John is approaching his Car. He is dressed like he is going to the Gym. Stapled to John's car door is a black and white photo of Lydia laying in a coffin. John pulls the photo out of his Car door which leaves a dent and two noticeable holes. Written across the picture in big black marker is: "Death Makes Angels."

EXT. JOHN'S APARTMENT BUILDING - DAY

John is talking to Detective Marx.

                    JOHN
          ...I mean, you guys have got to something!
          This bitch is seriously creeping me out!

                    DETECTIVE MARX
          Look, we've pretty much got everything we
          need at this point. We're gonna pick the
          girl up today.

                    JOHN
          Thank you! What a relief!

                    DETECTIVE MARX
          Okay, good luck to you. We'll be in
          touch.

INT. MONICA'S APARTMENT - DAY

                  JOHN
Are you almost ready?

                  MONICA (O.S.)
Almost!

She comes out of the bathroom and grabs her keys.

                  MONICA (CONT'D)
How are you feeling today?

                  JOHN
I'm good.

                  MONICA
Good. You ready for this?

                  JOHN
Yeah, let's go.

                  MONICA
Let's go.

INT. MONICA'S APARTMENT - DUSK

MONTAGE:

John and Monica sit on the futon watching TV John turns to look at Monica and they both start to laugh. John and Monica watch TV. A car speeds down the street and its headlights startle the pair. They trip like hell. It is very trippy. Yeah.

INT. MONICA'S APARTMENT - NIGHT

John and Monica lay on the bed side by side, John's feet by Monica's head.

                  JOHN
I'm not me.

MONICA
Who are you, then?

JOHN
I don't know anymore. I used to know. I used to create worlds. Now I just I show up.

MONICA
I'm afraid of surviving. The world's too big for simply surviving.

JOHN
I just want to live. I remember life. It was huge, it was so much bigger than me.

MONICA
When you're committed to your dreams they will come true. They give you life and the actions you take just happen naturally.

JOHN
Sometimes I still dream. And if you're dreaming...

MONICA
...you're fully alive.

INT. JOHN'S CAR - DAY

Monica and John are in the front seat with Methanie, Steve and Shawn in the back. They stop at a red light. Out of John's window we see a large ad which says: "Checker Moving Company -- The People Who Move."

METHANIE
So, uh John, how is Lydia doing?

JOHN
I don't know and I don't care. I haven't

heard from her since the cops picked her up.

> METHANIE
> Well, it all seamed to turn out well in the end.

> STEVE
> Except that part where she goes to jail and gets to be some bull dyke's bitch.

> JOHN
> Yeah. It's all good.

Steve pulls the car over outside John's apartment building.

John turns to Monica.

> JOHN (CONT'D)
> Are you sure you don't want to come in for a while?

> MONICA
> Not today sweets. I have some important stuff to work on. I'll come over tomorrow.

> JOHN
> Cool. See you all later.

John exits the car and waves to his friends as they drive away.

INT. JOHN'S APARTMENT - DAY

John sits down in front of his painting. We see paints being mixed, brushes coming out of a dusty box. John dips the brush into his palette, takes a deep breath and begins painting.

FADE TO BLACK

INT. HOUSE OF NINE - NIGHT

The night club is dark except for the narrow flashing lights. The music pounds. We find JOHN among the many Clubbers. John looks around the crowded club three girls catch his eye.

TAYLOR Stands against a railing. She looks at her watch and looks around as if she were waiting for someone.

LYDIA is sitting at a small table looking about hopefully.

ZINN stands by the bar looking frustrated and unapproachable. She looks like the demon lover that every man fantasizes about being with at least once in their lives.

John straitens his clothes and picks his way through the crowded club and towards Zinn.

    JOHN
So...uh, hi.

    ZINN
Hey.

She looks away as if she is completely uninterested. John looks over at Taylor who is talking to Janice. They begin to walk through the crowd and are soon lost in the sea of people.

    ZINN (CONT'D)
This club is pretty lame.

    JOHN
Uh...yeah I guess.

    ZINN

> My friend's band Ashfury was supposed to
> play here tonight.

The stage is empty. There is no band, no equipment, the band never showed. A stray power cord hangs over the edge.

ZINN (CONT'D)
> I paid the cover and everything and they're not even gonna play. I never pay cover.

JOHN
> So...I suppose you'll have to make the best of it.

ZINN
> Are you supposed to be the best of it?

John is taken aback, unsure of what to make of that.

JOHN
> My name's John.

ZINN
> I'm Zinn. Nice to make your acquaintance... Hey, do you have a car?

JOHN
> Yeah.

ZINN
> I know another club. It's pretty good. Would you like to go?

JOHN
> Uh-okay. What's it called?

ZINN
> I don't know - it's probably not going to be there long enough to have one. "Terror at the Opera" is going to be there.

> JOHN
> I've never heard of them.

> ZINN
> You'll love it. Lets go.

INT. JOHN'S CAR - NIGHT

Zinn is adjusting the radio.

> JOHN
> There are some discs under the seat. I have Nickelback, or...

> ZINN
> That's okay. Here put this in.

Zinn produces a single CD from her tiny purse and pops it into John's radio. Some very dark sounding music thumps tribally over John's cheap sound system. John's Blue economy car speeds down the road to the sounds of the music.

EXT. SPEAKEASY - NIGHT

A huge man stands outside of a door down a small alleyway.

There is no sign or distinguishing marks that say this run down building is a club.

> ZINN
> Uniform night.

The doorman gives an acknowledging grunt and opens the door and they go in. The same music that they listened to in the car is pounding as they walk down some stairs.

INT. SPEAK EASY FOYER - NIGHT

John and Zinn are instantly separated.

John looks a little out of place here. Suddenly John is grabbed around his chin like a mother might do to get the attention of her son. A small woman with bleach blonde hair, dressed like a small child, looks deep into JOHN'S eyes. John is shocked by the boldness of this girl to the point that he cannot move. Like a deer caught in headlights. She is obviously on some cocktail of drugs.

> GATE KEEPER
> You have the most courageous eyes I've ever seen. So engaging and virile. I've dreamt of these eyes for seven nights now and I have seen through

> GATE KEEPER
> (CONT'D)
> them. Come with me, I want to see them fuck.

INT. A DINGY BACK ROOM OF THE SPEAK EASY - NIGHT

Against the wall to the right is a small bed that could hold nothing bigger than a big baby doll. The gate keeper looks very amorously at John. The only light in the room hangs naked from the ceiling by a wire. It swings slowly.

> GATE KEEPER (CONT'D)
> You..are definitely...someone I would like to see around here more often. Now come here.. I want to use those eyes.

John walks over to the gate keeper. He kneels down in front of her so that his face is even with hers. He leans forward to kiss her but before he reaches her lips she falls over to the side. She has passes out. Drool runs down past her chin in a long string. John stands up and he looks as if he doesn't know what to do. He leaves the room in a rush.

INT. THE SPEAK EASY - NIGHT

John stumbles out of the dingy room.

                  ZINN
    Hi Greg, how's everything?

                  JOHN
    I'm having fun.

                  ZINN
    Why don't you give me ten dollars?

                  JOHN
    For what?

                  ZINN
    A gentleman would never ask.

John hands her ten dollars from his wallet.

She runs off. John grabs a shot from a girl walking by with a tray. He slams it. Zinn reemerges from the crowd.

                  ZINN (CONT'D)
    Things are dying down. Let's get out of
    here.

INT. JOHN'S BEDROOM - MORNING

John and Zinn are lying in bed, both fully clothed. It

Appears like nothing happened last night. The sun peaks through the window shade making all sorts of strange patterns that beam around the room. One of the rays hits John in the face jarring him from his sleep. John sleepily looks around. He sees Zinn and sighs. He gets up and pulls on his pants for work. He is moving very slow as if he is hurt all over. John begins to button his white dress shirt.

> ZINN

What time is it?

> JOHN

Almost 8:30, I'm running late.

> ZINN

Hey, Dave this is a nice place.

> JOHN

My names John, and thanks.

> ZINN

Oh, sorry John.

She stretches like a cat.

> ZINN (CONT'D)

What do you think of me?

> JOHN

I would do anything to see you tonight. Well, short of killing someone.

Zinn looks disappointed.

> ZINN

Damn.

> JOHN

Huh?

Zinn gets up and puts on her shoes.

> ZINN

What are you doing tonight?

> JOHN

Nothing...I think.

> ZINN

Would you like to get together later?

                    JOHN
          Yeah that would be great.

He looks at his watch.

                    JOHN (CONT'D)
          Oh shit! I gotta go.

INT. JOHN'S APARTMENT LIVING ROOM - DAY

John and Zinn are running for the door. John scoops up his jacket from the floor on the way.

                    ZINN
          I'll see you tonight around ten thirty.
          We'll start early.

John opens the door.

                    JOHN
          Okay. Hey, do you want to get together
          for lunch?

                    ZINN
          Are you kidding? I'm going home to sleep!

They leave through the door. The door closes.

INT. JOHN'S OFFICE BUILDING - MORNING

John is rushing toward the closing doors of the elevator.

                    JOHN
          Hold the door! Hold the door!

The doors open.

INT. JOHN'S OFFICE ELEVATOR - DAY

John enters the elevator and is greeted by Steve who is in the lift with two other gentleman and a lady.

The doors begin to close and John takes his place next to Steve.

                    STEVE
          You look like poo.

                    JOHN
          I was up all night. I met this amazing
          chick.

The woman in the back of the elevator coughs politely. John and Steve ignore her

                    JOHN (CONT'D)
          She's like... she's that demon lover you
          want to try at least once. Man, I want
          her!

                    STEVE
          You didn't tap that ass?!

The woman starts to look disgusted.

                    JOHN
          Not yet. I can't wait, though.

                    STEVE
          Is she goth?

                    JOHN
          I don't know. She's more than just that.

                    STEVE
          Leather and S&M? Or like some raver
          chick?

                    JOHN
          No, she's not like any of that. She's
          outside all that, somehow.

                    STEVE
          Could this be the one?

                    JOHN
          I hope so. She's so freakin' hot!

INT. JOHN'S APARTMENT-LIVING ROOM - NIGHT

John is picking up a bit. There is a knock at the
door. John answers the door and in walk Zinn, Brian,
and Methanie.

                    JOHN
          Hello...come in, uh, have a seat.

They flop down on the couch like they own the place.
John sits in a chair looking cautious.

                    JOHN (CONT'D)
          Can I get anyone anything?

John gestures to Methanie, who is sitting on Brian's
right.

                    JOHN (CONT'D)
          Beer?

                    METHANIE
          No, my boyfriend doesn't like it when I
          drink.

                    JOHN
              (to Brian.)
          Oh, you don't drink?

                    BRIAN
          I don't care if she drinks.

                    METHANIE
          Ha! Brian's not my boyfriend!

                    JOHN
          Uh, Brian...how about a beer?

                    BRIAN

Sure... Zinn's being rude. What's your name?

> **JOHN**
> John... Zinn can I get you something?

> **ZINN**
> No.

INT. JOHN'S APARTMENT KITCHEN - NIGHT

John walks in opens the refrigerator and grabs two bottles of brews.

INT. JOHN'S APARTMENT - NIGHT

Brian watches John go.

> **BRIAN**
> Nicely done, Zinn. Are you sure this guy's cool?

> **ZINN**
> Hey I got us a place - who cares if he's cool.

John is oblivious.

> **METHANIE (O.S.)**
> Can we smoke in here?

> **ZINN (O.S.)**
> You don't smoke do you John?

> **JOHN**
> No. But you can if you want.

INT. JOHN'S APARTMENT - NIGHT

John walks back into the living room and hands the beer to Brian. The three are all smoking cigarettes. John gestures at the table offscreen.

                        JOHN
            Is that what I think it is?

                        BRIAN
            Yeah, this is cool right?

                        JOHN
            Uh, yeah. Er, I've always kinda wanted to
            try it.

                        BRIAN
            Well, today's your lucky day.

John sits nervously. Zinn bends down offscreen
and comes back up, smiling like a shark. She
turns to John.

                        ZINN
            Take it you fuckin' wimp.

John Looks really nervous.

                        BRIAN
                  (To Zinn)
            Hey. That's enough.
                  (To John)
            This is your first time?

                        JOHN
            Yeah.

                        BRIAN
            Do you know what to expect?

                        JOHN
            Well yeah, I've heard lots of stories.

                        BRIAN
            Most of them are probably exaggerated.
            It's a very unique experience. If you
            take it cool and relax it can be very
            enjoyable.

> ZINN
> Just don't freak out!

> BRIAN
> Zinn, dearest... shut up.

Methanie snickers.

> BRIAN (CONT'D)
> Now, John you really have nothing to worry about. If you start to freak out just remember that it will do you no good and relax. Once you do this you have about six hours before you will be normal so there is no point in freaking out. If you don't want to do this you don't have to.

> JOHN
> No. I think I'll give it a try.

> BRIAN
> Okay, let's do it.

John ducks offscreen under the camera. Brian soon follows. The two come back into frame at the same time.

> BRIAN (CONT'D)
> Okay?

> JOHN
> Okay.

INT. JOHN'S LIVING ROOM - NIGHT, LATER

Brian, Zinn, Methanie, and John have just finished taking a hit. The three of them sit on the couch.

> ZINN
> Why don't you smoke?

> JOHN

I don't know. What is it about smoking?

                ZINN
Smoking is an expression of pleasure.
Tell him Brian.

                BRIAN
Smoking is an expression of pleasure.
    (beat)
Smoking a cigarette can be very
pleasurable. It can be sexy. It can
be relaxing. The thing is as soon as
you stop smoking for pleasure and start
smoking to feed an addiction all that
goes away and you start to look like an
asshole. There's nothing sexy about
addiction.

                ZINN
There's nothing sexy or relaxing about
standing outside in 7-degree weather
just to smoke anything. If food were
to suddenly be banned from buildings I
imagine those same people probably

            ZINN (CONT'D)
wouldn't go outside just to eat a snack.

                JOHN
So, when you start to feel addicted do you
stop doing it for a while?

                ZINN
I never deny myself any pleasure.
    (To Brian)
Unlike Mark. What an asshole...

                BRIAN
Ahh, Mark. We have a friend named Mark.
All of a sudden one day he decided to

start smoking. He went from not smoking one day to smoking a pack a day the next. When his co-workers went outside to smoke he started to go with them whether he wanted to smoke or not. He was determined to get hooked.

              ZINN
I think he set an alarm on the weekends so he could maintain his schedule.

              BRIAN
Mark thought there was some kind of comradery in addiction - that's what he was after.

              ZINN
Tragic, huh?

Brian rolls his eyes and turns to John.

              BRIAN
Are you feeling anything yet?

INT. JOHN'S LIVING ROOM - NIGHT

They are all sitting on the couch. Brian and the girls are all smoking cigarettes.

              JOHN
I still don't think I feel anything...
Wait a minute. Whoa!

John falls to his knees in front of the TV everyone gives him a snicker.

              METHANIE
I think he feels it.

INT. JOHN'S LIVING ROOM - NIGHT

Music plays softly and John is doing a flowing

free form dance with his arms. Brian is spelling something with stick matches on the coffee table. Zinn is dazed on the couch. Methanie sets down her cigarette in a cereal bowl turned ashtray and begins to dance with John. She approaches him from behind and puts her are around his torso. She flows with him.

INT. JOHN'S LIVING ROOM - NIGHT

John sits on the couch between Methanie and Zinn. Zinn has her leg stretched across John's lap she is looking at her pack of cigarettes. Methanie is leaning back against the cushion laughing quietly, like a lunatic, to herself, looking rather insane. On the coffee table written in match sticks is the word "unclean". Brian is nowhere we can see.

INT. JOHN'S APARTMENT - NIGHT

John is sitting rolling a small green rubber ball between his forefinger and the coffee table. He has a lit cigarette hanging from his mouth.

INT. JOHN'S APARTMENT - DAWN

John and Methanie are passionately making out on the couch. Still no Brian but now where's Zinn?

INT. JOHN'S BEDROOM - DAY

John and Methanie are naked in the bed. Methanie is lying on John's arm. They are sleeping. John stirs.

                    JOHN
     Huh? Ohhh shit.

Frustrated, John pushes his head down on the pillow. Methanie smiles in her sleep and rubs up to John.

                    METHANIE

Good morning.

                    JOHN
          Hey...
               (Beat)
          Where's Zinn?

                    METHANIE
          I think she left. You are really fun,
          John. You know that? I had a really good
          time last night.

John leans against the dresser and smiles.

INT. JOHN'S OFFICE ELEVATOR - MORNING

Steve is waiting in the elevator. The door begins to close. John is moving fast but not running toward the elevator. Steve pushes the "door open" button. John steps in. His shirt is open two buttons from the top. He is wearing no tie.

                    STEVE
          Wow, where were you this weekend? I
          called like twelve times.

                    JOHN
          I know. Sorry. It's just good to be back
          to work. I think I realized that I am no
          good out on my own. I need the structure
          of the work week.

                    STEVE
          What did you do?

                    JOHN
          In truth...I slept most of it. Friday was
          pretty wild though.

                    STEVE
          Oh!?

> JOHN
> Yeah, Zinn came over. She brought some friends. It was a party.

> STEVE
> Was your dialing hand broken? Why didn't you call me?

<Ping!> The elevator stops, the doors open and the two get off. The elevator doors close behind them.

INT. JOHN'S OFFICE - MORNING

John and Steve get off the elevator.

> JOHN
> These are not your kind of people.

> STEVE
> What do you mean?

> JOHN
> They're kind of sleazy.

> STEVE
> Sleazy can be fun.

> JOHN
> Yeah, but I don't think you're their kind of people. You're not sleazy enough.

They enter into their adjoining cubicals. Steve pops his head over the partition.

> STEVE
> Wow, that's the first time I've been called not sleazy enough. What are you doing Wednesday?

> JOHN
> I think we're going to see a movie.

                    STEVE
          A sleazy movie?

                    JOHN
          Shut up, you prick.

INT. JOHN'S CAR - NIGHT

John is in the back seat with Zinn. He is dressed
in all black. Brian is driving. Next to him
is Monica. Monica is wearing a "skinny puppy"
type long sleeved tee-shirt. She is smoking a
cigarette.

                    JOHN
               (Lighting a cigarette.)
          Zinn, you dress up all the time. What's
          up with that?

                    ZINN
          Well, I'll tell ya. When I was a little
          girl my mother used to scare me by saying
          if you make that face too much it will
          stick and you will have to look like that
          all the time. Later I thought, what if
          a light were to come from the sky and
          permanently tattoo what you were wearing
          to you. You know, like we wouldn't need
          clothes anymore. Ever since then it has
          always been important for me to dress
          well.

                    JOHN
          Oh.

A nice car pulls up beside them at a red light.

                    MONICA
          Check out the ride next door.

The light turns green and the girls, both sitting on the passenger side, roll down their windows.

EXT. JOHN'S CAR - NIGHT

The girls stick their heads and upper bodies dangerously out of the sedan.

INT. JOHN'S CAR - NIGHT

JOHN'S P.O.V. VERY DISTORTED AND WAVY.

The sound is also weird, very slow and long.

     ZINN
  You fucker, why'd you do it?

     MONICA
  You did it didn't you?!

INT. NICE CAR - NIGHT

The DRIVER looks around nervously. Sweat pours down his face. He looks toward the heap in his back seat covered by a blanket.

     DRIVER
  How do they know?

The car hits a small bump and a bloody arm falls out from under the blanket.

INT. BRIAN'S SEDAN - NIGHT

JOHN'S DRUGGED UP P.O.V.

The girls duck back into the Car. They are laughing.

     BRIAN
  Where the hell did that come from?

    BOTH GIRLS TOGETHER
  I don't know.

Both start laughing hysterically.

INT. BRIAN'S SEDAN - NIGHT

JOHN'S DRUGGED P.O.V.

Everyone is being quiet in the car. A "smooth" song drones in the back ground. John is looking out the window. Everything is surreal.

Zinn is playing with John's palm as if it was the most fascinating thing in the world.

EXT. HOUSE OF NINE - NIGHT

There is a long line to get in but the four don't care and just walk in.

INT. HOUSE OF NINE - NIGHT

JOHN'S DRUGGED P.O.V.

Lights dance and music thunders throughout the club. The crowd here all are dressed like Zinn and Brian. Methanie and her boyfriend Shawn approach John.

                    METHANIE
Hey! You luscious manly man!

                    JOHN
Huh? Oh hey, Meth.

They embrace.

                    METHANIE
John this is my boyfriend, Shawn.

John shakes Shawn's hand.

                    JOHN
Nice to meet you.

                    SHAWN

Meth tells me you're an animal!

                JOHN
Well, what can I say?

He laughs. The room spins.

INT. JOHN'S BEDROOM - MORNING

There is a large lump in John's bed that looks like it may be John sleeping but with a slick camera movement we see that John is actually sleeping on the floor and the lump is just a bunch of pillows. The telephone rings. John fumbles for it. Ring. John stands up to get a better view of the room. He stumbles. Ring. Just as it rings a fourth time John grabs the phone.

              JOHN'S MACHINE (O.S.)
Hello, this is John, I can't come to the phone, leave a message. <BEEP!>

                JOHN
Hold on the machine is on.

EXT. CAFE METROPOLIS - DAY

Steve is dressed for business but John is wearing the remains of his club outfit and a pair of shades. A few tables away Taylor is trying to wait on a table full of obnoxious goth brats.

                STEVE
What's going on with you, man? You haven't been to work all week.

                JOHN
I'm just surprised that I'm awake during the day.

                STEVE
What, are you turning into a vampire?

You're starting to dress the part. Work is not going to appreciate your new look.

              JOHN
Oh, well.

Taylor comes up to their table.

              TAYLOR
What can I get you gentlemen?

              STEVE
Mocha latte, please.

              JOHN
Coffee, black.

              TAYLOR
I'll be right back with your drinks.

John pulls out a cigarette and lights it.

              STEVE
Man, what are you doing?

              JOHN
I'm having a cigarette. What's it look like?

              STEVE
It looks like you're changing. Very fast.

John exhales and stares at the ceiling.

              JOHN
I know. But it's so much more exciting than going to work. It just feels right.

              STEVE
Who are these new people you're hanging out with? Why don't you bring them

around? Are you hiding me?

John takes a drag from his cigarette.

          JOHN
I'm not hiding you. These people are just very particular about who they are around.

          STEVE
And you don't think they would want to be around me?

          JOHN
That's not what I said. I'm just waiting until they are totally comfortable with me before I bring you out.

          STEVE
Will I have to start smoking? And...

          JOHN
Don't blame them. It's something I'm doing. You act like I never smoked before.

          STEVE
John, that's because you didn't.

          JOHN
You're so full of shit! That time beh...

          STEVE
We were thirteen! It's a little late for you to become a rebel.

          JOHN
Look I don't really think that you would fit in with these people.
            (beat)
They don't hang around people who still live with their fucking parents.

Steve's expression hardens.

                    STEVE
          You are an asshole.

                    JOHN
          Am I?

John puts his cigarette out.

                    JOHN (CONT'D)
          It's been good. Not great but good. See
          ya!

He leaves, bumping Taylor on the way out, sending their drinks to the ground. Steve just stands there shaking his head.

                                        FADE TO BLACK

INT. TANGENT GALLERY - NIGHT

The gallery is a plain white warehouse space with painting hung on the walls. There is a quiet party going on here.

John and Zinn walk in through the door. John puffs on a cigarette. The gate keeper is sitting on the couch talking with a young guy.

Among the small crowd and low din of sound is Holiday Martin, the independent filmmaker. Holiday stands conversing with two intellectual types, sipping her red wine.

Hand, dressed in a black turtle neck, breaks away from a crowd of older, more elegant party-goers. He walks over to Zinn who is standing with John, Monica, and Methanie. Behind him we see Brian talking to the elders, shaking hands and socializing. Zinn turns to Hand.

> HAND
> Hello, Zinn.

> ZINN
> Hello, Hand.

She slowly gives Hand a hug.

> ZINN (CONT'D)
> Oh, John this is Hand.

John shakes the hand of Hand. On the back of Hand's hand is a large round scar.

> JOHN
> Hey. Nice to meet you.

> HAND
> Likewise.

> ZINN
> (To Hand)
> Well, we're gonna get some drinks. See ya.

John and Zinn walk away. Zinn leaves John for another room. John looks at Holiday - Brian comes to stand by John.

> BRIAN
> Hey, John.

Brian looks at what John is looking at. Holiday.

> JOHN
> Brian, you fuckin' scared me.

John looks back at Holiday.

> JOHN (CONT'D)
> That girl over there. Who is she?

Brian looks as if he is about to speak but then stops.

JOHN (CONT'D)
What?

BRIAN
That, my living too much in the light friend, is Holiday Martin. She makes underground movies. She is also very beautiful.

JOHN
What do you mean by underground movies? Like, porn?

BRIAN
No, more like extremely gory stuff. Severed heads and bodies with the parts all mixed up. You know, family fare.

JOHN
Have you talked to her yet?

BRIAN
Not tonight. Why - are you interested?

JOHN
She's okay.

BRIAN
What do you mean "okay"? She is the devil's own angel. And she's looking...
(Beat)
...at you. Go for it.

John swallows hard.

JOHN
If Zinn comes back um, entertain her okay?

John begins to circle closer to Holiday. From the

side he is intercepted by Methanie, who is obviously altered. Methanie grabs him from the side in an aggressive hug, almost a tackle.

> METHANIE
> John! I love you. You know that don't you?

> JOHN
> Huh?

He looks toward Holiday, who is looking at him out of the corner of her eye.

> JOHN (CONT'D)
> Meth... hey.

They rub up against each other and she gives John a big bite on the neck. John smiles and warms up to Methanie.

> JOHN (CONT'D)
> Thanks. Hey, where's Shawn?

> METHANIE
> Out with his band tonight. But he said I could go home with anyone I want tonight.

John is distant. He looks through the sea of people that has formed between himself and Holiday.

> JOHN
> Uh, cool, hey I'll see you later. Okay?

John begins his maneuver through the crowd before Methanie can even answer. He finds himself suddenly standing right behind Holiday. He pauses, looking awkward and not knowing what course of action to take. Holiday is talking to two people, HOWARD and DAVE. She turns around very calmly and looks him straight in his eyes.

                        HOLIDAY
          And you are?

                         JOHN
          Huh?

She offers her hand and smiles.

                        HOLIDAY
          Hello, my name is Holiday. Are you always
          this well spoken?

John shakes her hand.

                         JOHN
          Uh...Um, John. Nice to meet you.

                        HOLIDAY
          Well John, we were just discussing
          something of great importance. I think
          we need the opinion of someone else.
              (Beat)
          Who would win in a fight: Macguyver or
          Boba Fett?

                         JOHN
          What?! Macguyver would get his ass
          kicked!! Boba fett would destroy him!

                        HOLIDAY
          See Howard, I told you he was smart.

                        HOWARD
          I don't know. I would put Macguyver up
          against Boba Fett. Just give him some
          baking soda, a stick of gum and duct tape
          and boom!

                         DAVE
          How about Boba Fett Verses the Leprechaun.

                        HOWARD

Shut up! You and that damned Leprechaun.

                    JOHN
Okay, I got one. Boba Fett Verses Danzig.

                    HOWARD AND HOLIDAY
Wow.

                    HOLIDAY
That's a tough one. Here's a classic.
How about Han Solo Verses Indiana Jones?

                    JOHN
Braveheart verses Chewbacca.

                    HOLIDAY
Braveheart verses Danzig.

                    JOHN
Roseanne Verses Worf!

                    HOLIDAY
Okay, C3PO verses Morrissey!

                    JOHN
Oh-uh... Michael Stipe.... ver...ah...
verses the snuggle bear!

JOHN'S P.O.V. SUDDENLY, HANDS COVER JOHN'S EYES

As if it was JOHN'S eyes, the camera is covered by two hands. Black.

                    GUS (O.S.)
Guess who?

                    JOHN
I hate this game. Who is it?

                    GUS (O.S.)
You have to guess.

                    JOHN
          I honestly don't know.

GUS takes his hands away from John's eyes. John
turns to see who it is. Gus looks disappointed.

                    GUS
          Sorry, I thought you were someone else.

John looks around but doesn't see Holiday anywhere.

                    JOHN
          Hey where did she go?

                    DAVE
          She had to use the little girls room.

                    JOHN
          Oh.

INT. THE TANGENT GALLERY - NIGHT

Glasses and other debris are scattered everywhere.
Most of the guests have left. John is sitting on the
couch by himself looking depressed. Brian sits down
on the couch.

                    BRIAN
          Hey, you're not mad about me and Zinn?
          You said to entertain her.

                    JOHN
          Huh? Oh, hey, No man, Zinn has already
          made it pretty clear she's not mine.

                    BRIAN
          Where's Holiday?

He lights a cigarette with his big Zippo lighter.

                    JOHN
          I don't know. She went to the bathroom.

I haven't seen her since.

> BRIAN
> Lets make like Zinn and blow - eh?

> JOHN
> Okay, it's not like I have to work tomorrow.

They begin to leave. Methanie, Monica, and Zinn Join them.

Zinn is straitening her clothes.

> BRIAN
> What do you mean?

> JOHN
> I lost my job today.

Brian and Zinn exchange a concerned look.

> BRIAN
> That sucks, huh?

> JOHN
> Oh, well. This is more like real life.

They leave. The door closes.

INT. CAFE - NIGHT

John, Brian, Methanie, Monica, and Zinn sit in the smoking section on a couch. They're all smoking. John clips on a barrette he found in the couch cushions.

> HOLIDAY (O.S.)
> I like your barrette.

> JOHN
> Uh...thanks.

Holiday is sitting on the couch next to John's.
Holiday is with Dave, Howard and the Gate Keeper.
John turns to face her.

> JOHN (CONT'D)
> Hey! How are you? Where did you go?

> HOLIDAY
> I'm fine. I'm here.

> JOHN
> Don't go anywhere. I really want to talk
> to you but I really have to pee.

> METHANIE (O.S.)
> You really pee a lot.

> JOHN
> Everyone's got to have a hobby.

John leaves to go to the bathroom. He passes Taylor carrying a coffee pot. John continues on his way without a word or even a look. The Gate Keeper pushes her way in next to Brian. She acts as if she knows him well.

> GATE KEEPER
> Hey Lover! Just thought I'd come over
> here and say hey!

> BRIAN
> Hey you.

> GATE KEEPER
> What are you doing with that fuckin' guy?

> BRIAN
> I don't know, he's got a good apartment.
> He's okay.

> METHANIE
> He's a good fuck.

                    BRIAN
          He lost his job, we'll have to find
          someone new soon.

                    ZINN
          Did Jamie's band play tonight?

                    GATE KEEPER
          How the fuck am I suppose to know? I was
          at the same party you were. Looks like
          you got some tonight.

                    ZINN
          Yeah? Jealous?

John saunters back from the bathroom. His hands rest
in the pockets of his dark pants. Holiday is too
busy reading her a small book to notice John's long
stare.

                    GATE KEEPER
          Here comes your fuck.

John sits. Everyone snickers.

                    JOHN
          What?

                    MONICA
          Nothing.

John notices that Howard and Dave are sitting at
another table with another guy. Annoyed he gets
up and sits at the table with Holiday. Holiday is
reading through a pamphlet about safe sex.

                    JOHN
          Greetings.

                    HOLIDAY
          Hello.

                    JOHN
          Is that interesting?

                    HOLIDAY
          Oh, it's jam-packed with helpful hints.

John laughs. Holiday produces a rose from what seems like nowhere and hands it to John.

                    HOLIDAY (CONT'D)
          I give this to you.

                    JOHN
          Does this mean I have deflowered you?

Holiday stares at him, blankly.

                    JOHN (CONT'D)
          No really, thanks.

Holiday sits still, not moving or laughing. She looks steadily into John's eyes. John looks uncomfortable. The moment is tense and weird. Then Holiday smiles.

                    HOLIDAY
          Listen buddy I'm sick of you and your
          little reindeer games.

She laughs. John looks a bit confused.

                    HOLIDAY (CONT'D)
          You're sarcastic. I like that in a boy.

                    JOHN
          Uh...do you want to walk with me?

                    HOLIDAY
          Okay.

EXT. METROPOLIS CAFE - NIGHT

The pavement shines as it has just rained. Very few cars are on the road this late at night. John and Holiday walk in silence for a moment. They pass under a rusted out train bridge. John looks up at it as they pass under the graphittied hulk.

>   JOHN
>   This city's something else.

>   HOLIDAY
>   I would say it's like nothing else.

>   JOHN
>   Murder capital of the world.

Holiday fixes him with an icy look.

>   HOLIDAY
>   Bad monkey. You missed the point.

John flushes with embarrassment.

>   JOHN
>   Wh... well what is said point?

>   HOLIDAY
>   Let me tell you something. I could live
>   in Amsterdam, or Paris, or New York, or
>   London, or a dozen other cities. But I
>   live right here.

>   JOHN
>   And why's that?

>   HOLIDAY
>   Because those cities are done. Their
>   histories are written. They produce some
>   good art, and the sushi's great, but it's
>   someone else's scene. Anything you do is
>   just another part of that scene.

>   JOHN

What do you mean?

                HOLIDAY
Did Rembrandt paint on DaVinci's canvases?

                JOHN
Uh.... no.

                HOLIDAY
No. Rembrandt painted on his very own empty canvases. And that's what Detroit is. My very own empty canvas. And your very own empty canvas. It's anyone's empty canvas if they have the brass to use it. And that's why it's like no place else right now. People

                HOLIDAY (CONT'D)
say it's a has-been city. I say it's a city between breaths. I say it's waiting. And what it's going to be is more amazing than what you or I can imagine.

They walk along is silence for a moment.

                JOHN
Do I have you?

                HOLIDAY
Do you have me?

                JOHN
Uh, yeah you know... uh, well... it was a stupid question.

Holiday blows it off.

                JOHN (CONT'D)
Do you give everyone flowers?

                HOLIDAY
No.

                    JOHN
          Why did you give one to me?

They stop under a big bridge, they turn and look at each other deeply.

                    HOLIDAY
          Can I tell you a story?

                    JOHN
          Yeah.

                    HOLIDAY
          Once upon a dark time, there was a
          beautiful girl and a handsome young man,
          I suppose not unlike myself and you. One
          day they went strolling in the deep woods.
          Holding hands while walking among the
          trees it began to rain. They sought and
          found shelter under a bridge, not unlike
          the one we are standing under now. The
          beautiful

                    HOLIDAY (CONT'D)
          girl looked up at the handsome young man,
          like so...

Holiday tilts her face toward John's.

                    HOLIDAY (CONT'D)
          ...and asked him to kiss her. Being a
          man burdened by virtue and restraint, he
          refused. At that moment lightning struck
          the bridge, sending it crashing down upon
          them. They were both killed instantly,
          their longing unfulfilled... Now, I don't
          know about you...but...I don't want to die
          like that.

                    JOHN
          Uh...Oh.

John kisses her. She returns it. A car screeches by. They abruptly stop.

> HOLIDAY
> Do you want to fuck me?

> JOHN
> Huh? I ...uh....I mean. That's not what I ....uh, I want more from you than just that.

> HOLIDAY
> You don't belong to those people, do you?

> JOHN
> What do you mean?

> HOLIDAY
> You're a normal guy aren't you? Why are you here?

> JOHN
> Fuck you!

Holiday simply smiles at him and pats him on the cheek.

> HOLIDAY
> There's my boy.

She hands him a small black card.

> HOLIDAY (CONT'D)
> My number. Call me if you feel... inspired.

John looks down at the card. It is glossy black card-stock with a stylized rose in one corner and a simple font stating "H. Martin - 313-666-1723"

INT. JOHN'S BEDROOM - NIGHT

Holiday's card sits next to John's phone, which is ringing. John's hand fumbles into frame, pulling the handset back O.S.

>   JOHN (O.S.)
>   Hello? BRIAN (phone) What are you doing?
>   It's almost 10! Are you going diurnal on
>   us?

>   JOHN (O.S.) (CONT'D)
>   Wh... no! What's on the menu tonight?

>   BRIAN
>   (Phone) Club, then chill at my place. Be
>   there or square.

The phone hums as Brian hangs up. We hear John getting up, grabbing his keys, etc. while staying on the phone and Holiday's card. The door closes and there is a moment of silence before we hear John come back. His hand reaches into frame and grabs Holiday's card.

INT. MONICA AND BRIAN'S APARTMENT - NIGHT

The front door is slightly ajar. A sliver of light shines in from the hallway beyond. There are scraping sounds, and heavy breathing. From outside the door we hear Brian, John, and company stagger in.

Into the hallway. They've obviously been partying it up.

>   BRIAN
>   Hold the... her foot's stuck in the...

Methanie giggles.

>   JOHN
>   That's her elbow!

Raucous laughter erupts as the light from outside is

blocked off. They stop just outside the door.

                    BRIAN
          What the... Everyone shut up!

Brian pushes the door open, he seems to sober up
instantly. Brian pushes the door open. He is
holding up a very altered, very unconscious Zinn.
John, Shawn, Monica, and Methanie stand next to him.

                    BRIAN (CONT'D)
          Whoever's in there is in some deep,
          painful shit.

Brian simply drops Zinn. She hits the floor like a
sack of potatoes. Methanie giggles again. Brian
flips on the lights. His eyes widen.

                    BRIAN (CONT'D)
          Mark! What the hell do you...

Suddenly the front door slams in Brian's face.
John's eyes widen as he sees a hastily improvised
noose hanging in the closet doorway.

                    BRIAN (CONT'D)
          Mark! Open! This! Door!

                    MARK
          Stay the fuck away from me!

                    JOHN
          He's gonna hang himself!

Brian bangs futility on the door.

                    BRIAN
          Open the door, Goddamn it!

We hear a phone dialing.

                    MARK

> Screw you assholes! You started it here,
> and I'm ending here! All of it!

> JOHN
> Where's the key?!

Inside we here Mark talking into the phone.

> MARK
> Taylor? Listen... Shut up! Just listen!
> Listen for once!

Brian is rooting around on his keyring, trying one key after the other.

> SHAWN
> Hurry!

> MARK
> Tell Mom and Dad I tried. What the fuck
> else did they expect?! I tried, okay?!

> METHANIE
> Mark, come out! Get out of there!

> MARK
> All of you shut up! You had your chance!

> BRIAN
> Damn it!

Brian gets the door open - Mark has chained the door shut. Brian throws down his keys and reaches in, trying to get the chain open.

> MARK
> Tay it's not you. It's not you. It's
>   (screaming through the door)
> These useless fucks! These fucking
> leeches! You ruined my life and now I'm
> ruining yours!

JOHN
Brian...

Brian is still trying to get the chain open.

BRIAN
I know.

JOHN
He's gonna do it!

BRIAN
I know!

MARK
Bye, Taylor. I love you.

We hear a phone hit the floor inside.

JOHN
Fuck it!

John pushes everyone aside and kicks the door. It buckles in its frame but doesn't give.

METHANIE
John, hurry!

Two more kicks and door flies open.

INT. BRIAN'S APARTMENT - NIGHT

The door flies open. We see the back of Mark's head in the foreground, obscuring part of the doorway. He unmoving.

Everything is still. Everyone stares, frozen for a moment.

BRIAN
Jesus Christ.

INT. HALLWAY OUTSIDE BRIAN'S APARTMENT - NIGHT

We see Holiday's card, held up to John's cell phone as he dials her number. It rings for a bit as John holds it up to his ear. Detective Marx ushers two men in white coats into the apartment. The phone rings for a bit. Someone picks up, but says nothing.

                    JOHN
Hello.... hello?

Silence on the other end. John looks at his phone as if to make sure it's working.

                    JOHN (CONT'D)
Holiday?

Holiday chuckles on the other end.

                    HOLIDAY
Feeling inspired?

                    JOHN
Inspired isn't the word for it. I'm over at Brian's. The cops are here.

                    HOLIDAY
Oooo... cops. Tell me you've been bad.

                    JOHN
Not especially. One of the guys here killed himself.

                    HOLIDAY
Anyone I know?

                    JOHN
Guy named Mark.

Holiday snorts in disgust.

                    HOLIDAY

That little shit! I told him to call me before he snuffed it.

                    JOHN
          Don't beat yourself up, I guess he was
          pretty far gone. Nobody could have
          stopped him.

                    HOLIDAY
          Who said anything about stopping him? I
          just wanted to get a few cameras rolling
          when he did it. A few nights ago I let
          him whine at me for almost an hour before
          he agreed to call me first.

John is speechless, taken aback.

                    HOLIDAY (CONT'D)
          So, did you just call to torment me with
          missed opportunities? Or are you offering
          up an alternative?

John raises an eyebrow.

INT. HOLIDAY'S APARTMENT - NIGHT

The door opens. John is standing outside. Holiday gestures him in. A big bed with iron posts rests against the wall. Unlit candles are everywhere even on the floor. Video and film equipment sit in neat piles in the corner. Holiday grabs John, slams him against the wall. She grabs him by the throat and kisses him deeply. He gathers his wits and returns the kiss.

                    HOLIDAY
          Do you want some wine?

                    JOHN
          Uh...yeah, sure. Okay.

Holiday retrieves and open bottle from the

refrigerator and pours a glass.

INT. HOLIDAY'S APARTMENT - NIGHT

Holiday is busy lighting candles and incense all over the room. John comes out of the bathroom.

> HOLIDAY
> Your wine is next to the bed.

> JOHN
> (Notices only one glass.)
> You're not having any?

> HOLIDAY
> (Her best Dracula)
> I never drink...wine.

> JOHN
> I think you're evil.

> HOLIDAY
> Do you?

> JOHN
> Yeah. But I think that's sexy. Evil turns me on.

Holiday finishes lighting candles and sits on the bed next to John.

> JOHN (CONT'D)
> So what do we do now?

> HOLIDAY
> Oh, I believe we'll think of something.

She tackles John like a cat taking a mouse.

INT. HOLIDAY'S APARTMENT - NIGHT

John is lying naked on the bed, his extremities

conveniently covered by the horribly disheveled
sheets. He looks very content. Candles are the
only light but they are everywhere. The room looks
exactly the way we left it before, though the candles
are burned a little more. C.U. of John's face and
shoulders. He takes a deep sighing breath. John
Closes his eyes just for a moment. She kisses him
before shifting herself next to him. She kisses his
elbow.

                   HOLIDAY
   You have the sexiest elbows.

John laughs. Holiday sits on the bed Indian style
with the sheet covering her sexy parts. Light dances
around her body from the many candles. Holiday runs
her finger along John's back. John turns on his side
to look at her.

                   JOHN
   I love it when you smile. I wish you
   would do it more often.

Holiday's smile goes away.

                   HOLIDAY
   Well...

John reaches into the drawer and pulls out a stick
of incense and lights it. He then lays down Facing
away from holiday but toward us. The smoke drifts
in front of John's face. Holiday Hangs herself over
John's flank with her head on her hands.

                 HOLIDAY (CONT'D)
   You know if you don't kiss me now the...
   Ceiling will crash down on us, killing us
   where we lay.

John laughs and kisses her. Gets on top of John and
forces his hands down.

                    HOLIDAY (CONT'D)
            You're mine now sucker!

John flashes with excitement. He grabs holiday
and forces himself on top of her, Reversing the
situation.

                        JOHN
            I'm not so easy!

Holiday, now on the bottom. Her look of surprise
is quickly replaced with a smile. She then slowly
begins to rise. This forces John to go up as well.
John looks surprised by her apparent strength and
retaliates with all of his might. Despite John's
full weight on her, Holiday prevails with an amazing
display of feminine power and puts John onto his back
so his feet are facing the headboard.

                    JOHN (CONT'D)
            I am yours!

INT. HOLIDAY'S APARTMENT - EARLY MORNING

Holiday is sitting on the edge of the bed. She is
looking out the window very intently. The sun is
gradually devouring the shadow on the floor. John
wakes up and kisses her shoulder.

                        JOHN
            Is everything okay?

                      HOLIDAY
                    (Whispers)
            Yes.

                        JOHN
            What are you doing?

                      HOLIDAY
                    (Whispers)
            Waiting.

                    JOHN
          Waiting for what?

Holiday Waits for a while before answering.

                    HOLIDAY
          I want you to fuck me. I want you to get
          me off. Make me cum? Will you?

                    JOHN
          Yeah.

                    HOLIDAY
          Good.

What follows is utter and total confusion. Fast.
Lots of quick cuts and close up shots. Holiday grabs
John and thrusts him - hard - onto the solid floor.
John's head slams down, he is stunned. His right
arm is stretched out long. Holiday uses the weight
of her leg to keep it in place. She drives a nail
through John's hand. The same is then done to his
left arm. Holiday goes down on John. After a few
seconds of this she mounts him. John is making a
lot of intense faces. Pain or pleasure? Who knows?
Holiday is going totally crazy as she bounces around,
using John like a doll. After a minute of this
she makes a loud screaming sound then suddenly and
abruptly she gets up and walks away.

JOHN'S P.O.V. IT'S SIDEWAYS, THE SAME WAY HIS HEAD IS
LAYING ON THE FLOOR.

Holiday walks, naked, across the room to a camera
aimed toward them on a tripod. A RED LIGHT BLINKS
AT JOHN. She takes THE CAMERA from the tripod and
moves around John aiming it at him. While she is
taping him all is quiet except for him breathing and
Holidays feet moving on the floor.

HOLIDAYS CAMERA P.O.V.

The sunlight from the window reaches across John's face, shinning off his eyes. Small puddles of blood have formed around John's Hands. She puts the camera down and kisses John on the lips.

> HOLIDAY (CONT'D)
> Thanks, I think I got some good shots. I am so glad that Brian told me about you. I am glad he wanted Zinn for himself. Do you want to go see a movie today?

John Passes out. Blackness.

EXT. JOHN'S APARTMENT BUILDING - DAWN

A box of junk is plunked down in a dumpster. A bandaged hand reaches out to tape the "Bored Beyond Belief" sign to the stuff.

INT. JOHN'S APARTMENT - DAWN

John walks up to his half-finished painting and applies a thick layer of gesso to the canvas, whiting it out. He winces a bit at the pain in his bandaged hands, but starts painting on the canvas anew as we pull out, showing his apartment to be empty of everything except his easel and paints.

INT. HOUSE OF NINE - NIGHT

The night club is dark except for the narrow flashing lights. The music pounds. We find JOHN among the many Clubbers. John looks around the crowded club three girls catch his eye.

TAYLOR Stands against a railing. She looks at her watch and looks around as if she were waiting for someone.

LYDIA is sitting at a small table looking about hopefully.

ZINN stands by the bar looking frustrated and
unapproachable. She looks like the demon lover that
every man fantasizes about being with at least once
in their lives.

John straitens his clothes and...   ...heads strait
for the door. He simply leaves the club.